Lou

Memoir of the Rev. Erskine J. Hawes

SALZWASSER
VERLAG

Louisa Fisher Hawes

Memoir of the Rev. Erskine J. Hawes

Reprint of the original, first published in 1863.

1st Edition 2022 | ISBN: 978-3-37500-118-6

Verlag (Publisher): Salzwasser Verlag GmbH, Zeilweg 44, 60439 Frankfurt, Deutschland
Vertretungsberechtigt (Authorized to represent): E. Roepke, Zeilweg 44, 60439 Frankfurt, Deutschland
Druck (Print): Books on Demand GmbH, In de Tarpen 42, 22848 Norderstedt, Deutschland

MEMOIR

OF THE

Rev. ERSKINE J. HAWES,

Pastor of the Congregational Church, Plymouth, Conn.

BY

HIS MOTHER

NEW YORK:

1863.

Engd. by A.H. Ritchie.

Erskine J. Hawes

CONTENTS.

CHAPTER VII.

CHAPTER VIII.

CHAPTER IX.

CHAPTER X.

CHAPTER XI.

NOTICE.

A MOTHER'S love, perhaps a mother's partiality, has prepared, and now gives to the public, this memoir of a deceased son.

The father has had doubts whether there were incidents in his life of sufficient interest to justify adding another to the numerous volumes of the same general character, already before the public. He felt the same doubts in regard to the memoir of his daughter, Mrs. Mary E. Van Lennep. He was happily disappointed then, and hopes he may be now. It has greatly mitigated the bitterness of bereavement in the loss of the daughter, to believe, as he is constrained to believe, that she did her work for good in the world, by her early death. Her memoir has been widely read, and has been of great use to many whom she could never have reached by any other influence.

And should this prove true in any good degree in regard to the memoir of the son, it would lighten much a sorrow which the lapse of time has but little relieved, and cheer a path from which the last light has been struck out. It was natural for the parents to desire, that brother and sister, so closely related in life and who were called away from their spheres of usefulness in the morning of their days, and in circumstances so affecting, should be associated with each other in a brief memoir, which should preserve and endear their memories for a time among their friends, and add something to their influence for good, when, like all earthly things, their names will be forgotten.

So let it be, since the hearts that loved them best, are consoled in the sweet hope that their names are found in the Lamb's book of life.

CHAPTER I.

BIRTH AND INCIDENTS OF CHILDHOOD.

Erskine Joel Hawes, the third son and the sixth and last child of the Rev. Joel Hawes, D. D., of Hartford, Connecticut, and of Louisa, his wife, was born July 23d, 1828, and died July 8th, 1860.

Of the six children just alluded to, four sleep with him, in the same enclosure, in the north burying ground in Hartford, among the people of his father's charge.

One,* the second, sleeps far away "among the Moslem dead." There, on the banks of the village-bordered and beautiful Bosphorus, the remains of this lovely young Christian rest, in hope of the resurrection of the just.†

* Mrs. Mary E. Van Lennep. † Evangelist.

As the subject of this memoir was closing his eyes upon earth, he seemed to catch a glimpse of the glorious "prospects" beyond. As they opened on the other side, is there not reason to believe it was to behold the vision realized. And amid that innumerable throng, would not this loved and sainted one, who had labored and prayed while here on earth, for the salvation of this now redeemed brother, be among the first to welcome him to that blest assembly?

The eldest of the six, Louisa,* died at the age of four years and one month—a sweet bud of promise, and having something more than simply being a "little child" to entitle her to a place among those of whom the Saviour has said, "of such is the kingdom of heaven." And was she not there, also—once a little lamb, carried in the Saviour's bosom, but now matured and shining in the beauty of holiness—was she not there to welcome the brother whom she had never seen on earth, to listen to

* "Louisa, My First-Born."—S. S. Union; Philadelphia.

the hallelujahs of heaven, as the plaudit "*well done*" was heard from the lips of the Master, welcoming the young disciple to the presence and joy of his Lord.

After the birth of Erskine, his mother was visited with severe and protracted illness, and the little boy was removed from home and placed where he could have that nourishment which the state of his mother's health prevented her from affording him.

At the age of one year and three months he was returned home. His mother had seldom seen him while absent, and he looked upon her as a stranger. In vain she attempted to attach the little boy to herself. The dissimilarity in age and appearance between herself and his foster-mother added greatly to the difficulty of doing this. Whenever she put him down on the carpet, he would make for a table on the further side of the room, and, creeping under, would stretch up his little neck so as to hide his face behind the drop-leaf, and would sit there like a timid and frightened dove, until drawn from his hiding-place by the sound of his father's voice; he being the only adult in the family who was not a stranger to him.

It was a pitiful sound to hear his moanings for his foster-mother. The eagerness with which he would watch the door as it opened, and the look of disappointment that would come over his young face, on not seeing the loved and longed-for one enter, told, more forcibly than words could have done, the *heart-sickness* within. At length this gradually wore away, but not without leaving its traces upon his character. It was, doubtless, owing to these frequent disappointments at this early age that he had so little of the element of hopefulness to cheer him through life. It also left its impress upon the countenance. A shade of melancholy was often observable, alternating with the smiles, in his most joyous moods. A little brother, who was nearly four years old at the time he was brought home, and whose death occurred one year and four months from that time, was almost constantly in school, as was also an elder and only sister, so that the little fellow was dependent almost entirely, at first, on his mother for occupation and amusement. When he became older—could talk, and run about by himself on the premises, it was soon apparent that he had a mind of very great activity, and also very fruitful in contriving amusements for himself, some of which were not free from mischief. A nest of kittens in the wood-house had to be watched very carefully, lest he should make too free use of them for playthings. One morning, his mother heard him trundling his little wheelbarrow with great swiftness over the flagging in the back-yard. On looking out, she saw the little things flying out on each side, in consequence of the heavy jolting over the stones, and that he was picking them up and throwing them in again. Calling out to him, she exclaimed, "What *are* you doing?" He replied, "I only giving kitties an airing;" probably in imitation of the "airing" to which he had been accustomed in his own little carriage.

Some time after this, his mother on seeing him enter the wood-house, followed as soon as she conveniently could, to see what he was doing there. The place where the little brood was, had been boarded up, so that he could not reach them. He had contrived to climb over, and finding that he could not climb back again with a kitten in his hands, he had tied a string around the neck of one, the other end of which he had fastened to the belt around his waist. With his prize, he had just touched the floor as his mother reached him; but the string having caught on a nail, the little thing hung dangling by its neck, and would soon have perished if she had not been by to rescue it. He had been made to understand that it would hurt the little things to throw them down upon the floor, and he had contrived this method to get one over without hurting it.

But though he would "not hurt the little kitty," yet the haste he made in attempting to disengage the one in the string, and his frightened look, as his mother approached, told clearly that he was doing something which he knew she would not like to have him do. He knew also that the boards had been put there for the purpose of keeping him from them.

Another experiment with the kittens, and we will dismiss them, though much sooner than he did his interest in them, and his endeavors to amuse himself with them.

When the little things had grown, and become strong enough to protect themselves, "with the pins in their feet," they were taken from their place of confinement, and permitted to run about freely.

One day when the little boy had been missing for a short time, search being made for him, he was found by the sink, in the kitchen. As his mother approached he stood perfectly still, looking very demurely into a kettle, from which the steam was rising. His mother perceived that water was dripping from the bottom of his clothes. On going round to ascertain the cause, she found that he was holding a little kitten by the neck, all dripping wet, and very closely down by his side, to prevent her seeing it. Instantly the truth flashed upon her mind, and plunging her hand into the water to ascertain its heat, she exclaimed, "what *have* you been doing?"

"I only been giving kitty a bath," was the reply.

He had been made familiar with the operation of the bath on his own person, but of the effects of water, heated above a particular point, he had no knowledge. Fortunately, the heat was not sufficient to do any harm in the present case, but the attempt that he made, to hide the kitten from his mother, showed that he felt he was doing something which she would think was wrong.

At this time he had never been burned, so that he had no knowledge of the effects of fire, except of its warmth, as was soon ascertained.

A few days after the affair of the bath, an exceedingly bright coal, surrounded by some very white ashes, on the parlor hearth, attracted his attention. Suddenly he darted towards it, and before his mother could prevent, had seized it between his thumb and finger. Instantly dropping it, he exclaimed, "O, I warm my thumb," "I warm my thumb," his tone and look affording abundant evidence of the torture he was then enduring. He might have taken the shining thing for a star, having once earnestly begged his mother to get him one.

That scene is still fresh in memory. It was in the autumn, the season when the bright star known as Capella shone conspicuously in the North East; just then, at the hour for his retiring. He had preceded his mother, and when she reached him, was standing by a north window at the head of the stairs, gazing intently at the brilliant object. Pointing towards it, he exclaimed, "Mother, do get a ladder and climb up there"—and "Tare the world down"—do "Get me that star." There certainly was a striking resemblance between the coal, shining amidst its pearly surroundings, and that particular star—there was also something in his look and manner, as he darted forward to get it, which seemed to say, "Now I've got you."

But whatever might be true in regard to this, the *burn* proved a very useful lesson. It, no doubt, saved him from a more dangerous experiment with that destructive element.

These facts, although unimportant in themselves, are introduced as specimens of numerous others of a like kind, to show that it required no small amount of patient and persevering effort, and no little ingenuity, to furnish suitable occupation for such an active, busy little being.

When he was three years and nine months old, his father went abroad and was absent several months. Thinking to cheer him, on the reception of each letter, his mother showed him the name at the bottom for him to kiss. At length, after repeated acts of the kind, he could bear it no longer. Holding the letter in his hand, with that emphasis of tone and manner which only real earnestness can give, he exclaimed, "*I* don't want any more *paper papa*, I want *my own papa;* why don't he *come home?*" Of course the practice was discontinued.

The little boy had now become tenderly attached to his mother. There was also another source of comfort left to cheer him in the absence of the *one* whom *now* he loved best of all. This was the sister spoken of in the commencement of this memoir. She was now ten years old, and it was her delight to aid her mother in the care of the little boy. The long summer days were never too long for this. The "sunshine and fair earth" were made to contribute to the furtherance of her plans. They were the capital, the store-house, from which she drew her resources. With her little brother she would roam over the fields and groves, listening to the song of the birds, or the murmur of the waterfall, uniting her own sweet voice with the ever-varying cadences of nature. A pebble, a clump of moss, a flower, or even a variegated leaf, were to her far richer sources of enjoyment than the most costly toy.

It was, doubtless, owing to the bent given to his mind, at this early formative period, that he ever after had such a high appreciation of the beauties of nature. As he advanced in life, his stores of pebbles and shells, and minerals and fossils, were treasured with the greatest care. One of the last things his sister did for him was to gather chalcedony for his cabinet among the rocks on the mountains of Asia Minor, near Smyrna, and pebbles and shells from the shores of the Euxine and the Marmora.

He had a fine voice, and his sister delighted in uniting it with her own in songs and hymns suited to his tender age.

He early discovered a fondness for the pencil, and would take sketches from the objects around him with considerable accuracy.

When quite young his father took him to Saybrook. On his return home his voice was heard calling for his mother. On finding her, he threw his cap on the sofa and taking from the crown a pencil sketch said, "There, mother, there is the meeting-house Pa preached in," —then another, "That is the house we stayed in." And the meeting-house and parsonage at Saybrook were recognized at once. A third which he produced was somewhat remarkable for a boy of his tender years. It was a good, if not accurate outline of the opening of Connecticut river into the Sound, with the landing at Saybrook, and Lyme in the distance. As his mother could not accompany them, he had made a special effort to show her how it looked there.

At a suitable age he was furnished with a drawing-master, and made fair progress in the art. Had he travelled abroad, as he hoped and expected to do, he would have found it an invaluable accomplishment. It often furnished him with pleasant occupation, in the absence of books and other things, when unexpectedly detained for a half-hour on a journey, or from other causes deprived for a short time of "*anything to do.*" With his pencil and a stray leaf from his pocket-book he would sketch something from memory, if there was no object of interest within sight. But, to return to earlier years.

At the age of five years he was sent to school. But, here, unfortunately, the method of instruction was not simple enough for his childish mind. Particularly was this true in regard to Arithmetic. His mother was not aware that this study had been given him until after several months, in which he had endeavored, though in vain, to understand its mysteries. At length, he asked her one day what it meant, "*to carry one for every ten;*" and she found that long sums had been given him with this single direction, *to* "*add up, and carry one for every ten.*" At this time he contracted a distaste for Arithmetic, which was a disadvantage to him through life. But, although it was not a study to his taste, yet when it was taken up in a more intelligent manner in later years, he proved himself no dolt in that branch of knowledge.

Geometry was little more than a pastime with him. This was a study just adapted to the character of his mind, which, when searching for proof in any case, never could rest satisfied with anything short of certainty.

At the time of his entering college, it had but just been added to the list of studies in the preparatory course; he was, therefore, obliged to take it up alone at home, a little previous to his entrance.

His mother recalls with pleasure the delight he experienced, in the satisfactory nature of its demonstrations, in which he often called on her to participate.

The year after leaving college he had a very fine class in Geometry in the high school. His pupils will not readily forget the charm he threw around their recitations.

CHAPTER II.

ENTERS THE GRAMMAR SCHOOL IN THE SPRING OF 1837.—INCIDENTS OF LIFE, DEVELOPMENT OF TALENTS, AND ATTAINMENTS FOR THE NEXT SEVEN YEARS.

SOMETIME during his tenth year, he was placed in the grammar school and commenced his classical studies. In these, and also the common English branches, he was a fair scholar; but in English composition he excelled. It was not unusual for him to bring his theme, nicely folded, to his mother, and ask her to lay it up; assigning as a reason that his teacher had told him to preserve it, as he might wish to look at it, at some future time.

Those early school-days furnish many a grateful reminiscence to the mother of the orderly conduct of her son, of his fidelity in study, of his careful observance of the rules of the school, and of the course he took whenever he had violated one. A single specimen, and the earliest remembered, shall be cited here, which may serve for every instance of the kind during the entire period of his school-days.

On passing through the kitchen, one morning, his mother found him sitting by the fire, apparently in deep thought and looking very sober. On her return he was still there. Perceiving him in trouble, she lingered a little, to see if he would speak to her about it. Looking up, he said, "Mother, I want to ask your advice."

"Well, my son, about what?"

"I have violated one of the rules of the school."

The mother's heart beat rather quicker than usual, but she waited in silence to hear his account of the matter, which was this:—

"As I was going to the post-office this morning, for father, I felt a snow-ball come pat into the back of my neck. Quick as thought, I caught up another, and sent it back. Just then

I saw Mr. —— (the principal of the school) at a little distance. He was not looking at me then, but I think he must have seen me."

"Well, what if he did? What harm in that?"

"He has made it a rule that the boys shall not snow-ball in the street."

"Then you have clearly violated that rule."

"What had I better do?"

"What had you thought of doing, my son?"

"I thought I would go early, and tell Mr. —— about it, and ask him to excuse me."

This was done. At noon Erskine returned, with a bright face, and said to his mother, "It was well I went. Mr. —— saw me. He said he should certainly have called me up before the school; but that now he should excuse me."

This little incident illustrates a prominent feature in his character—the readiness and propriety with which he made acknowledgment of any offense or wrong to those to whom he thought such acknowledgment due. To some this may appear a small matter; but, constituted as he was—modest, diffident, timid to an extreme—it required an amount of courage far greater than would be necessary in one differently constituted.

This diffidence was often a source of real suffering to him. A single instance shall serve for many others.

A lady, with whom he boarded, on his first settlement in the ministry, speaking to him one day of the frost, said she thought a little piece written by Miss Gould, commencing,

"The Frost looked forth, one clear, cold night,"

was the prettiest thing of the kind she had ever seen. He looked up, with a peculiar smile, and said, "*I detest it.*" To her look of inquiry he said, "It was the first piece I ever undertook to speak in public. I was five or six years old. My mother had taken great pains to help me prepare to say it well. I had learned it perfectly. I came forward on the stage at the school exhibition, made my bow, said one line, and then, thinking how many eyes were upon me, I burst into tears and could go no further. With the lines I always connect that mortifying scene and what I then suffered."

From that time, not only every allusion to the lines, but also to the freaks of that element, was carefully avoided. Even the delicate tracery on the window-pane, which had afforded him so much delight, now became to him so many instruments of torture.

This diffidence cost him many a hard struggle to overcome; but by the time he entered his teens he had so far conquered it as not only to speak with ease to himself, but to do this in a piece of his own composing. His mother has a vivid recollection of the scene, as he came forward upon the stage, with a manly air, but with a blanched cheek, at the public exhibition of the grammar school. The subject was one every way suited to his taste—"Ancient Ruins"—at the close of which a few lines, quoted from Macauley's "Pompeii," were pronounced with decided effect.

A little incident of his school-days may be here related, on account of its moral bearing upon his character.

Soon after he entered the grammar school, a fair was announced to be held in one of the public halls in the city. Erskine had the promise of attending, if he would get all his lessons.

When the day came, his mother handed him the note containing the request to the teacher to excuse him for a part of the afternoon. Instead of taking it, he said, "Mother, I can't go to the fair."

"What is the reason, my son? Have you not got your lessons?"

"Yes, ma'am," but I forgot to put down *my number four*. My teacher has made it a rule that, if the boys do not put down their numbers, they shall be punished just the same as if they had not got their lessons. I have got to stay till school is out, and an hour after." Here the little fellow broke down. Up to this point he had tried to be very manly, but he could stand it no longer.

Knowing that her son recited to an under-teacher, his mother wrote a note to the principal of the school, requesting him to remit a part of the penalty for that afternoon, and let her son take it at some other time, that he might have half an hour for the fair.

On going to the hall, his mother saw the little boy, with the principal of the school, ascending the same staircase with herself. On entering, he made his way through the crowd, to his mother, and, casting a very grateful look back at the principal, said, "He said I might come."

The principal immediately stepped forward, and said, aside, to the mother, that the rule was a very strange one; that he knew nothing of it until that afternoon; he should see that it was righted; "after a boy had got his lessons perfectly, he should not be punished for not giving himself credit for it."

The sunshine in the little boy's sky was brighter, that afternoon, for the shower that had preceded it. Instead of only the one hour which his mother had promised him, he had the whole afternoon.

He learned one lesson at that time, more effectually than he could ever have been taught it by oral precept—that, when a good was promised him on certain conditions, *it did make a difference whether he complied with those conditions or not*, present appearances to the contrary, notwithstanding. True, he could not reason in this manner in so many words; but the moral effect was the same on his character. He had that intuitive sense of right which is common to children who are not misled by false principles in their training.

On entering the grammar school he was thrown into the society of boys, most of whom were older than himself, and among them some whose moral training had been very different from his own. Their influence over him was decidedly bad, particularly in this respect:—they made an impression on his mind that it was not manly to ask mother's permission to unite with them in certain things, of which he doubted her approval. At first, the mischief was so slight as to be hardly perceptible. When it was at length discovered, it had taken such firm hold of his too yielding nature, as to require much vigilant and patient effort before it could be entirely eradicated. The one thing which made it so hard for the little fellow to free himself from the influence of the bad boys, was the fear of their ridicule.

His sister was at this time spending the winter at New Haven. When informed by her mother that her brother was becoming less docile and confiding than formerly, she immediately united her efforts, with those of her mother's, for the correction of the evil.

A specimen or two of her letters will show her happy and winning way with him, not only at this time, but during all the time from his early childhood, until she left him at the age of fifteen for her eastern home:

"New Haven, *November* 1, 1838.

"I could not pass you by, my dear little brother, but, when writing to all the others, I must send you a letter also. I think of you very often, and when Wednesday afternoon comes, I say, 'now Erskine has got to speak, and I fear he will be frightened.' You have to go to school alone, now that Mr. G—— is gone, but I hope you will be a very good boy and study your lessons hard.

"You must write to sister, my dear brother, for you know how glad she would be to receive a letter from you. Have you written any more compositions? When you write to me, tell me what subjects you have written about.

"Have you drawn any more Turks, dancing? I do not draw much now, but sometimes I take my pencil and sketch a little. You draw much more than I do, and will get along better than myself. I shall expect to see many pretty pictures when I return home—pretty landscapes, for I think you draw those better than you do figures or flowers.*

* When a little further advanced, he sketched natural scenery with a very bold and free hand, but he particularly excelled in drawing animals.

"I play much upon the piano, and we have some very fine music, and I often wish I could hear your sweet voice; but when I return we can again sing together many charming pieces.

"I wonder whether you have grown any—have become more like a man, and can understand your lessons better. I hope my dear brother is improving very fast in becoming good, and kind, and amiable. I see here some sweet little boys, who are very obliging and kind, and every one thinks well of them. My dear brother must try to be obliging and kind, and make every one feel pleasantly around him. This is the way to live happily in the world."

Again she writes, February 26th:

"And now, my dear brother, I sit down to thank you for your sweet note. It is becoming warmer, so that now you can walk out and enjoy the fresh air. Spring, with its soft winds and sweet flowers will soon be here, and then I shall be at home to walk with you. What nice times we shall have! I shall have many things to tell you about what I have seen and heard, and you will have much to tell me. When I come home I shall expect to find you quite a good Latin scholar. You must study hard, then you will understand very fast. But, my dear brother, when you are filling your mind with useful knowledge, you must take care that the tall weeds do not grow in your heart. Do you know what this means? The tall weeds are the bad, wicked feelings, and you must try to pull them out and have good, pleasant things in your heart.

"From your affectionate and *only* sister,

MARY."

BRIEF SKETCH OF THE AMUSEMENTS AND OCCUPATIONS OF HIS EARLY YEARS.

These were such as are common to children reared in the city, with very few of those fine invigorating sports, with which children in the country are favored, and which contribute so much to health and hardihood of constitution. Instead of the haystacks to tumble over in the fresh mown fields, and the lambs to frisk about with in the green pastures, he had only the block-house, and the tiny animals in Noah's Ark, with other little *et ceteras*, on the parlor carpet; and the miniature boat, with a tub of water for his *sea*, in an outer room. Instead of the long range of hard, smooth crust on the hill side, and the broad, strong sled, on which an elder brother or sister could sit and hold him in safety, as it glided swiftly down the smooth surface away into the valley, any little garden slope, on which his gaily painted craft could slide for a few yards, must serve for his sled ride in the city. Then he had none of those long jolting rides in the hay-cart, for which his smooth cushioned drives in a city carriage were but a poor substitute.

But such recreations as the parents could command were furnished in no stinted measure.

His ball, kite, and fishing rod, in summer, and the building of his snow forts and houses, to be demolished with missiles of the same material, with his skating and occasional coasting, in winter, served to keep him in such health as to enable him to continue his studies, though not as profitably as he might have done in other circumstances.

As soon as he was strong enough to handle the shovel and the spade, he had the additional exercise of clearing the snow from the walks around the house, digging over the few feet of ground for garden vegetables, and keeping these free from weeds; he also rendered essential aid in the care of his father's stable.

The mention of his gardening recalls vividly to the mind scenes long associated in memory with those early days.

He was occasionally indulged during the long days in his summer vacations with an excursion to the Talcott Mountain, one of the range forming the western boundary of the valley of the Connecticut. This was always a great event with him. The prospect from the tower erected on its summit; the smooth sheet of water enclosed, almost entirely, within its high, rocky embankment; the beautiful lawn sloping down to the edge of the lake, on that side left open to the view, as if to disclose its peaceful resting-place within; the small though tasteful dwelling, used by the owner of the grounds as a summer residence, between which and the lake were fruit and forest trees interspersed in graceful variety, with many flowering vines and shrubs, both wild and cultivated; the deep ravines, and the eminences from which a new view was gained at every turn; all these combined to form in the mind of this young enthusiast, a picture little short of the Elysian fields.

But it was not merely the picture here described that was suggested to the mind, by the mention of his gardening—it was something more beautiful than that—it was his delicate remembrance of his mother. Those clumps of wild columbine, with their gay flowers of scarlet and yellow, occupying any little spare nook in a corner of his garden beds, and the field violets, which even now continue to bloom among the grass—it was the memory of something associated with these frail emblems, but more imperishable than they, that was thus called up before the mind. On returning at one time from *his day* on the mountain, the basket that had carried out his lunch was filled with wild flowers. Taking them out with their roots firmly attached, the earth around them being well saturated with water from the lake,

"*I brought these home for you.*"

It was this delicate expression of sympathy and affection, from the son to his mother, that was so suddenly called up and clothed anew with life, by the mention of one of the early occupations of his childhood.

It might have been owing to the fact of his mother's having been so much of the time his sole companion, while his tastes and habits were forming, that whenever he had any unusual enjoyment he wanted her to participate in it. Especially was this true during his mountain rambles. He knew how much she enjoyed fine scenery—he could not bring *that* home to her, but he could the flowers—he knew how much she loved them. In the instance narrated, instead of cutting and tying them into a bouquet as usual, he patiently disengaged the roots, leaving enough of the soil to protect them, until he could transplant them into the garden at home.

As he advanced in years, and entered upon a severer course of study, it became necessary to furnish him with additional, and more vigorous exercise. For this purpose, his father had a work-bench erected for him in an outer room in the back part of the house, and procured for him a complete set of joiners' tools; with these, and material to practice upon, he soon developed a fine mechanical genius.

After he had become accustomed to the use of tools, he undertook a work which required much artistic skill—the constructing an electrical machine. For this, he had no pattern, only the plates, description, and directions for making, found in the Edinburgh Encyclopedia, in his father's library. This not only furnished him with employment, but kept his mind in a state of healthful excitement during the winter of 1843–4, when he was left with his mother, his father having accompanied his only sister to her home in a foreign land. At length all the parts were finished and nicely adjusted to each other, and the machine stood up—no inferior model of its kind. The whole, with the exception of a little assistance at the smithery, and the turning lathe, his own workmanship. It was a powerful machine. Of this he had soon a practical demonstration. Having charged his jar at one time very highly, he took the whole shock into his arm. The inflammation caused by the electric fluid was so great, that it was necessary to resort to medical aid in order to reduce it.

The next effort was, the constructing a *camera obscura.* This he made use of in sketching scenes near home, to send to his sister abroad. These were a source of much enjoyment to her; while looking upon them, she imagined herself again walking in the old familiar streets, or entering the houses, the doors of which were standing open to receive her.

Next, a *magic lantern* occupied his leisure hours. Then a *solar microscope*, each of which displayed much skill and answered well the use for which it was intended.

But his highest enjoyment was in music. When he was a little boy he always had two or three Jews-harps on hand; and an Æolian harp of his own constructing, showed no little ingenuity. At one time, the table bell was missing; when searched for, it was found suspended in the wood-house, with a little wheel, taken from his tin cart, and a long cord attached, so that it could be rung after the manner of the bell that called him each morning to school. Soon after entering his teens, his father furnished him with a flute. In the use of this long coveted instrument, he found, not only much enjoyment himself, but also gave much to others. One of his friends had a very fine-toned violin, and an evening or two in each week was spent in practicing together some piece adapted to the two instruments. As they were good performers, and their pieces selected with care, the two friends made no indifferent music. Those strains, as they come floating along down the vale of time, seem to the ear of memory, like some sweet, solemn requiem for the departed. But with them comes also a more joyous *refrain*, bringing the consoling hope, that, though lost to earth, another strain has been added to the minstrelsy of the heavenly choir, another voice, to those of

"The glowing seraphs round the throne."

In addition to these evenings with this friend, he often joined in larger circles of instrumental music during the few years preceding his entering college. In these he took great delight.

But there was one instrument, exquisitely tuned, the work, not of human skill, to which he resorted oftenest, and with greatest pleasure. For improvement in the use of this he had many facilities; at first in the juvenile singing school and concert. His voice, which at this time was a clear, high soprano, fitted him to take a prominent part in the latter, but such was his diffidence, that he could seldom be induced to perform a piece alone. His sister had early learned to read music, and when he began to use his voice in singing, she could do much for its improvement.

When his voice became settled, as it did in maturer age, into a deep, rich, smooth bass, he took his place in the choir in his father's church. He was a leader for a part of the time, at least, in the college choir, and the same office was assigned him in the Theological Seminary. In short, wherever he was, as a pupil, a teacher, a student in college, in the Theological Seminary, he was always known as sympathizing deeply in all musical improvements.

After his settlement in the ministry, his interest in this divine art knew no abatement. He found a very fine choir in his own church, and he delighted in encouraging them by his presence in their musical gatherings.

One of the members of his church, in a letter of condolence to his parents, speaks thus of this prominent accomplishment in their youthful pastor:

"Your dear son was an enthusiastic lover of music. Often has he met at our dwelling in the happy circle of the lovers of sacred song, uniting with them with heartfelt pleasure and delight. And when from around that sacred spot where rest his precious remains, the notes of that delightful song ascended on high, resounding among the spreading branches of that grove, it seemed as if his redeemed and happy spirit must be hovering above, uniting in the sweet harmony with heavenly rapture."

Another member of his church remarked, "As I have looked at him while pouring forth his rich voice, I have often been reminded of a remark I once heard Mr. Hart* make of a very good singer:—I love to look at him while singing, and think what music he will make in heaven."

* A former beloved pastor of that church.

CHAPTER III.

PREVENTED ENTERING COLLEGE BY THE STATE OF HIS HEALTH — LIFE ON A FARM—SIX MONTHS IN WILLISTON ACADEMY.

At seventeen years of age he was fitted for college. He had also paid some attention to the French language, and had made fair progress in its attainment, when his health failed, and he was obliged to discontinue his studies for a time.

His classmates entered college, and he was left behind. This was a great trial to him at the time, but it was afterward viewed by him in a very different light. When, at the age of nineteen, he did enter, he felt that he had a much better appreciation of the privileges of a collegiate course, and that he was qualified to make a much better use of those privileges, than if he had entered at an earlier period.

The summer of 1845 was spent upon a farm

in the country. Before entering upon his new employment, he procured a treatise on agriculture, and studied it thoroughly. He knew that he was entirely ignorant of the business of farming. True, he could use the shovel and the hoe, the garden rake and spade; but of the uses of the field implements he knew nothing. Then, he was ignorant of the nature of soils, of the best manner of making them productive, in short, of everything relating to the cultivation of a farm. The knowledge he thus acquired was of great use when he entered upon the practical part of the employment. The gentleman, on whose farm he worked, said that he took hold like a farmer, and that he would have done as much work as his hired man, if he had allowed him to do it.

The pains he took in qualifying himself for his new employment, strikingly illustrates one of his prominent characteristics—never to undertake anything until he was quite sure he could do it well. This he afterwards carried to such an extreme, as greatly to impede his usefulness, and at one time threatened to destroy it entirely.

He had nearly concluded his theological studies, and was soon to appear before the public as a candidate for the pulpit. Up to this time, his father had never been able to obtain from him a single extemporaneous effort. He continued his theological studies for more than a year after having received his license to preach. He had occasionally delivered a written discourse in the lecture room, had read the hymns and offered the prayers, but more than this, he could never be persuaded to do. His father became discouraged.

On his mother's remonstrating with him on his unwillingness to comply with his father's wishes, he very gravely assigned this as the reason: "*I have made up my mind that I will never do anything that I cannot do well.*"

"Then," my son, was his mother's reply, "*You may make up your mind that you will never do anything.* You will never certainly know that you can do a thing well until you try, and you will never try, at the risk of making a blunder; so you see, that you will never do anything."

This *sage resolution*, he found it expedient to modify; a measure for which he was afterwards truly grateful, when called to off-hand, extemporaneous efforts among his own people. At the time of his settlement in the ministry, he had acquired so much ease and readiness in these, that his people regarded them as the most interesting and efficient of his public performances.

But to return to the farm.

Of his employment on the farm, he writes thus to his father:

"I have been very busy, helping about hoeing corn and potatoes, making hay, binding and stacking rye, boring holes in rocks for blasting, making wells, with a variety of other things. Making hay is nothing but sport. But boring holes in rocks and hoeing corn is hard work. I have sometimes worked more than half a day on a single rock, but there is, nevertheless, much satisfaction in seeing the hard iron rock blown to pieces with gunpowder." Of his studies he writes, "I am very much pleased with your suggestion about reading, and generally contrive to read a little every day. I am studying Sallust in order to keep up my memory of Latin. I find my knowledge of that classic is considerably refreshed by helping J—— about his lessons. At Mr. L.'s suggestion we have made a contract, I am to assist him in his Latin, and he again is to give me a few hints about farming."

Of his recreation, he writes thus to his mother:

"Besides farming, there will be plenty of other sport here. There are two trout brooks about a mile or two out of the place, and I intend sometime, in company with J., with Mr. L.'s permission, to pay them a visit. Such visits, though, I suppose will be very rare, and I intend they shall be.

"I hope also to visit the 'hanging hills.' I

can see the range distinctly from my window, and I intend, some time, to make a drawing of them and send you."

His love of the beautiful in nature lost none of its ardor while laboring on the farm. Of this, his letters home gave abundant proof.

To his mother:

"Since I have been here I have had many pleasant rides. Last evening I had a most delightful one. The moon was shining brightly, gilding the tops of the mountains and trees. The house where I stopped was situated in a most romantic place, and, a few rods from it, a brook ran gurgling and splashing by; while, far down in the glen, I heard for the first time, the clear, protracted, silvery notes of the 'whip-poor-will,' uttering that word so plainly that it seemed to proceed from the human voice. It was one of the most pleasant and delightful spots I was ever in, and I can give you but a faint description of it."

One more extract from his letters home, will

close the account of this, to him, so pleasant and profitable a summer.

"A few days ago, I went with J., and the hired man, to Prospect on the mountains, to gather blackberries; and we were amply repaid, not only in the quantity of fruit we gathered, but also in the fine prospect which everywhere lay spread out before us. The scenery wanted neither rocks nor mountains to give it a sublime and bold appearance, nor fields nor meadows to give it beauty, nor spires, villages and country seats, to give it variety, but all these combined together, formed a most magnificent panorama."

In the month of September, he returned home much invigorated in body and mind, and, as he said, "all toughened up and ready for study."

In the month of December, 1846, he entered Williston Academy. This was merely an experiment to ascertain whether he had the requisite health to pursue a collegiate course and enter upon a professional life.

The experiment proved successful, and after a six-months' residence, in which he made many friends, and gained for himself a fair reputation for scholarship, and an enviable one for gentlemanly and correct moral deportment, he returned home.

The mountains in the vicinity of Easthampton furnished him with a fine opportunity of indulging his taste for natural scenery. During his residence there he made two excursions to Mount Tom. The first, in the month of December, shortly after his entrance to the seminary, he thus describes in his letters home:

"Last Saturday, in company with a few others, I made the ascent of Mount Tom, and I must tell you what an adventure I had of it. I suppose you will think me very foolish and venturesome; and, I must confess, I think so myself.

"In the afternoon, seven of us started for the mountain, one carrying a hatchet, another some matches with which to build a fire on the summit, for it was very cold and the wind blew very hard.

"After walking about two miles, we came to the foot of the mountain. Now, the regular way would be to go around a portion of it and ascend in that way, but one of our party, for the sake of the name of it, proposed to make a bold push straight up the steep side, and, as it were, take the mountain by storm. This was strongly objected to by some of us, but we were finally influenced by the rest to make the attempt. So up we went; at one time on all fours, at another, grasping some shrub or some projecting rock. The mountain was covered with snow, and a crust having formed over it, this gave some security to our feet. Soon the party separated, each striking out a different course for himself. There was a gully extending quite up the mountain and filled with snow. I took the gully, but soon began to repent of this, as the snow was quite deep, and the footing quite precarious. To add to my trouble, my hands became numb, so that I could scarcely grasp anything that came in my way, and one of my limbs became cramped.

"At last I had arrived to within about a hundred feet of the top, and was thinking with some satisfaction that I should soon be there, when, on looking around, I saw on each side, two almost perpendicular barriers of rock, and also that the gully was filled with ice, which was so slippery that I could proceed no further. I must confess that I was a little frightened at my situation, for I was almost exhausted. After deliberating a little, I raised my voice, and called as loud as I could. It was some time before I could make myself heard. The party had now reached the top. At length, one of them put his head over the ravine and just caught a glimpse of mine. After some consultation, it was decided that the only way for me was to slide down on my back the same way that I came, and so I did, expecting all the while to have my neck broken: but after I had gone some distance in this way, I began rather to like the motion, until I tore my clothes, which was not quite so pleasant. In my descent, I slid about two hundred feet, and certainly I never had, nor ever want to have, such a slide again. Finally, I once more found myself on firm footing, and making the ascent in the tracks of the others. I need not tell you that I was very much wearied, and do not know what I should have done, had not one of my companions come to my assistance. By taking hold of his hand, and grasping the rocks, and now and then a tree, I at last managed to gain the top, but so exhausted I could scarcely stand. After having warmed myself by a good roaring fire, and dried my wet stockings and gloves, I regained my strength and spirits, and could look around with infinite pleasure on the almost unbounded panorama on either side of me. You can not conceive what a sublime and beautiful view it was. I could see, away off in the distance, the faint though marked outline of old Monadnock, many other bold mountains appearing on every side. But the most interesting part of the view was that which lay all along the winding Connecticut, which we could distinctly trace almost as far as Hartford. Indeed, it being a very clear day, we thought we could see Hartford, away in the distance, as far as the eye could reach. We could also see distinctly East and West Rock in New Haven, and the bold juts of the Berlin and Meriden range. I need not tell you that I was the most interested in the prospect which lay to the south."

As the spring opened, in a letter to his mother, among more important items, is this little episode:—

"A few days ago, while poring over my algebra, I heard the first blue-bird singing to the rising sun, on a tree directly in front of my window. What a thrill the first note of this harbinger of spring sent through me. In a moment my mind was diverted from my dry lesson, and went roaming over green meadows, and purling brooks, and up the mountain side, and where else I cannot say. Now I know just what you are thinking of. 'If

Erskine allows his mind to be diverted from his studies by the simple song of a blue-bird, he will not accomplish much this term.' But I must excuse myself by saying, the mind often works better after some such diversion by way of change, but it would not do to have too many such diversions."

In the month of April he made a second ascent up the same mountain, but "so changed was the aspect of nature, that it hardly seemed like the same."

His own account of this to his mother: "Last week I made a second visit to Mount Tom, but the auspices under which I visited it, this time, were far different from those before.

"The snow had all disappeared, and we made the ascent by the customary path. The day was very fine, and with the aid of a good glass we saw many objects of interest. Right under our feet, flowed the beautiful Connecticut, having its smooth surface broken by the rapids at Hadley Falls. We could almost look into the windows of the seminary at South Hadley, and see Miss Lyon surrounded by her pupils. Turning our glass in the direction of Springfield, we saw distinctly the flag on the United States Arsenal, the cars at the dépôt, with many other striking objects; we could follow the Connecticut almost as far as Hartford, as it gracefully flowed on through its beautiful valley. Still farther south, lay the bold Berlin and Meriden mountains, and with our glass we got a glimpse of Wadsworth's Tower, on the Talcot range. But there was one thing, on which I gazed oftenest, with intense interest—and what was that? Away as far as the eye could reach, nearly on the horizon, could be seen, a minute spot of light; with the aid of the glass, this light spot was transformed into the tapering spires of my dear old Hartford. It was Hartford, undoubtedly, for I counted its seven prominent steeples, and could even discern the dark Episcopal tower. It fairly made me feel homesick. Well, school closes in four weeks, and then I shall find myself no more in

Easthampton, but again participating in the pleasures of home."

While at Easthampton, he gained some knowledge of life which was of use to him afterwards. As might be supposed from the previous brief sketch of his character, he had no relish for practical jokes, and he never intended or expected to have anything to do with them. But on his first entering the school boarding-house, where were several pupils besides himself, he got drawn into two or three of these.

One of the pupils, not over scrupulous in his observance of the rules of the school, and noticing the exactness with which Erskine observed them, determined to make him violate one, at least, if possible. He soon found opportunity for doing this. Having borrowed something of Erskine, which he knew would be needed during the hour of study, when all the pupils were required to be in their rooms, he purposely avoided returning it. When Erskine went to him for it, he suddenly shut the door, locked it, and putting the key in his pocket, said, "Now, you are not going down till the study hour is over." Erskine finding that remonstrance was vain, and not thinking it best to attempt obtaining the key by force, as in that case the house would be disturbed, and he would be required to report unfavorably of the offender, yielded as best he could to the "*durance vile,*" until such time as his jailor saw fit to liberate him. His generous and gentlemanly conduct at this time, gained for him the respect of all to whom the transaction became known.

He now found it necessary to be continually on his guard, lest he should be drawn into a participation in some foolish prank, planned by the idle and restless for the annoyance of the more studious of the pupils.

On passing through an upper hall one morning, two of the pupils, who were pulling with all their might upon a rope, called out to him to stop. On hearing the request, "Hawes, lend us a hand here," he turned back, and, not noticing that the rope was fastened to a door knob, and that the door opened inward, he grasped it with both hands. Instantly they fled, when the door yielding to the force applied on the inside, opened with a bound, and out sprang the infuriated pupil, who had been thus kept there against his will, and, with clenched fists, darted upon his innocent victim. Instantly they fell—the pupil, restraining, as by magic, the intended blow, exclaimed, with a voice, agitated by the sudden revulsion of feeling, "Hawes, if I had not seen that it was you, I should have felled you to the floor." An apology was of course made, which set the matter right. Erskine had now gained for himself so much respect among his fellow pupils, that he was not afterwards molested. He had also gained what he afterwards found occasion for, in his college life—"courage to be thought *simple*, concerning evil."

A few remarks here seem to be demanded to correct a mistake that will very naturally be made on reading the foregoing pages, viz., That it was really easy for him to do right, easier than the contrary. This was far from being true. Could all the struggles he was obliged to make to extricate himself in the hour of temptation, be recounted here, they would be seen to be no mere child's play. The thing which, more than any other, was instrumental in keeping him from being swept away, if not utterly ruined, by the temptations with which his path was beset, at every stage, from infancy to manhood, was his confidence in his mother.

To a kind Providence it was owing that this one link in the chain which bound him to a life of virtue and usefulness, was never broken.

In September, 1847, he entered Yale College. It was with much uncertainty as to his being able to continue his studies, that he entered on his collegiate course, but contrary to his own fears, and also those of his friends, his health was much better during the four years of his college life, than at any previous period of the same length. This was doubtless mainly owing to the climate—its proximity to the sea; but something must be attributed to the regularity of his college life. As must have been seen, he had a great dread of being found delinquent.

With his customary forethought, he provided against the possibility of this, in regard to his college exercises.

The boarding-house selected for him was at some distance from the college, and out of hearing of the college bell. His mother, at his request, placed herself near the chapel, watch in hand, while he passed to and from his boarding place, that so he might time the distance. The same forethought and precision entered into all his arrangements.

His first visit home, was at the annual Thanksgiving, November, 1847. He met his mother at the door, and with a beaming countenance said, "Mother, I have *done it*," alluding to something which she had been exceedingly desirous to have him do, but to which he had manifested great reluctance.

To the cordial welcome of his father, he responded in such a way as to show that it was not undeserved. "Father, I have not been late to prayers, nor absent from prayers, *once.* I have not lost a lesson, nor had a poor lesson, *once.*" These things were said, not in the spirit of boasting, but to assure his parents that he had not been unmindful of the privileges they had conferred upon him, but had improved them to the extent of his power. That was truly a thanksgiving visit.

Here was one secret of his uniform health, a cheerfulness resulting from the consciousness of doing right.

CHAPTER IV.

RELIGIOUS TRAINING—PROFESSION OF RELIGION —COLLEGE LIFE—YEAR IN TEACHING.

Although the whole course of his training, moral and intellectual, was aimed to be conducted on strictly Christian principles, yet there were times when the great doctrines and duties of religion were brought to bear more immediately on the mind and heart.

As soon as the little one could take in the idea of *One* who lived above the sky, of a heavenly Father there, he was taught to address to him little petitions in simple words, in order to awaken, in his yet unformed mind, a sense of his dependence upon him, as also of his accountability to him for all his conduct.

During this early period, a scene is remembered, with a distinctness and vividness as if of yesterday's occurrence.

It was sometimes necessary for the mother

to take her little boy with her, during her hour for retirement. At such times a quantity of toys would be placed before him, in some pleasant part of the room, while his mother retired to some more secluded spot. On one such occasion his little feet were heard patting softly along to the chair where his mother was kneeling. Having laid his head upon it he continued looking wistfully up into her face, until she laid her hand upon his forehead and invoked for him the blessing of his heavenly Father. Those soft eyes! they seem to be looking up into that mother's face now, she would fain hope not reproachfully! But oh, what a moment was that, when the young, the immortal spirit of the little one, was taking the direction of its flight for eternity.

The scene never rises before the mind, without the most overwhelming sense of a mother's responsibility in shaping the immortal destiny of her child, and the necessity that is laid upon her, *to see to it*, that nothing be wanting on her part, to secure to the little one, committed to her care for that very purpose, an immortality of blessedness.

From this time onward, as his mind opened to the reception of ideas, he was instructed in the simple elements of divine truth, the basis of which was, the fallen and ruined state of man, and his recovery to the favor and friendship of God, through the mediation and suffering of Jesus Christ. Such instruction was never given him in a cold, formal way.

The simple stories of the Bible, the familiar hymn, such as "Watts' Divine Songs," and other attractive methods, were adopted to draw his young heart away from the world, and lead him to seek his happiness in the love and service of God. But although his mind was often deeply impressed by divine truth, particularly truths relating to his own condition as a lost sinner, exposed to eternal death, and as often during childhood was pointed to him who said, "Suffer little children to come unto me," and in maturer age, to "The Lamb of God, who taketh away the sins of the world," yet something kept his young heart back from God, and his parents were made painfully to feel the necessity of divine interposition in his behalf.

Soon after entering the grammar school, he was greatly distressed about himself. He felt that he was a sinner, needing pardon and peace with God, and cried out in anguish of spirit, "Oh, mother, what shall I do?" And what could his mother tell him to do, but to commit himself to *Him*, who only could do for him what he needed.

At this time he asked his father to "let him stay out of school a *little while*, as he could not be good there."

The expression of countenance, indicating the struggle within, the tone of voice, the manner of that touching, child-like request, seem still present to the mind of the writer.

As time passed on, he had frequent seasons of deep anxiety about himself. At the age of seventeen, at which time, as has been seen, the failure of his health prevented his entering college, he was in a state of alarming despondency, threatening at times, his intellect. For months previous to his going on to a farm in the country, he suffered more than words can express, from a fear of having committed the unpardonable sin; at this time, it was common for him to resist sleep, lest he should wake in the world of despair. He would often say to his mother, he was "a poor worthless being, only an incumbrance in the world, and the sooner he was out of it the better."

All the promises of the Gospel were powerless then. They failed to throw one ray of light athwart hs clouded vision. It was useless also to point to the state of his health, as one cause of the state of his mind. The only thing that kept him from absolute despair, was, the confident faith of his mother, that God had a work for her son to do in the world, and that, by this discipline, he was qualifiying him for the performance of it.

This belief of hers she labored to impress upon his mind, by every means in her power, and it so far availed as to awaken in him a hope that it might prove true. The following lines vividly describe his state at this time:

"I see, or think I see,
A glimmering from afar,
A beam of day that shines for me,
To save me from despair."

After his summer on a farm, and his winter at Easthampton, his health was much improved, and his mind in a much better state.

He had lost none of his interest in the subject of religion, but he looked at it in a calmer and more hopeful manner. He could now contemplate his personal interest in it without that desponding feeling, which had, hitherto, prevented a successful prosecution of the subject whenever it had pressed with more than usual weight on his mind.

As the time drew nigh for him to enter college, he quickened his efforts to become a Christian, yet he entered with the conviction that he was not at that time "all right" in regard to that important matter.

When in college, he found that there were temptations to encounter, of which he had formed only the faintest conception. This put him upon looking up for strength to resist, and overcome them. It had been his habit from childhood, to resort to prayer, in any case of trial. It is believed that he never retired at night without committing himself to God in prayer. While at Easthampton, having taken up a higher, and of course more difficult branch of mathematics, after having detailed some of his difficulties to his mother, he continues, "I pray over my studies, and I don't see that they come any easier to me." But to resume the subject of his interest in religion.

On his return home during the winter vacation, January, 1848, there was a marked change in his views and feelings in regard to the subject of religion. He was more hopeful, and could converse with calmness on his own interest in the matter. It was evident that the one subject uppermost in his thoughts, and to which all the energies of his mind were directed, was the securing an interest in Christ, and the blessings of his salvation.

On his return to college at the close of the vacation, he soon communicated to his parents the grateful intelligence that he "had the pleasing assurance of having made his peace with God," and that he "had at last found rest in the bosom of his Saviour."

He spoke of his "previous indecision," of "the wavering state of his mind," of having "been balancing the question, whether to give himself entirely up to God or not." He continues, "On Sunday evening last, when returning from chapel, I made the firm resolve *to give myself thenceforth and forever to God*, and I went to my room feeling very happy, and endeavored to strengthen, by as fervent a prayer as possible, the resolution I had just made." * * * In this letter, he speaks of "a sermon on the Judgment, by President Wheeler," which he had heard some time previous; in which, the final judgment was held forth in such a light, as to make a deep impression on his mind, that ever since that time he had been thinking more and more seriously on the subject. He says, "Perhaps it would be well for me to remark here, that all the time I have been in New Haven, I have had my thoughts turned more to the subject of religion than before, and there seems to have been an influence here, which I have never before felt." * * * *

One who had known Erskine from childhood, had spent some years in his father's family, had partly fitted for college there, and who is now a minister of the Gospel, in a letter to the mother of Erskine, says:

"On the day that your beloved daughter, Mrs. Van Lennep, left Hartford, I said to her, 'Oh, I wish Erskine was a Christian, it would be such a comfort to you now.' 'Charles,' she replied, 'I know he will be converted. I have prayed to God for him, and I am perfectly sure that Erskine will become a Christian.'

"I often thought of those words, and longed for the event, for they inspirited me with the result. When Erskine came to Yale, I was rejoiced to see that he had full confidence in me as a friend, and came to me for help and counsel. At a proper time I spoke to him of personal religion, to which he listened with earnest attention, said he thought much on the subject, and knew he ought to be a Christian.

"One Sabbath afternoon, the last in January, 1848, as I sat in my room lost in reflection, arising from the sermon I had just heard in the chapel, a gentle knock aroused me from my reverie. Erskine entered, and in a moment I saw by the look of anxiety on his face that he was in great trouble. I said, 'Well, Erskine, how is it about your soul?' He burst into tears and said, 'Oh, Charles, I am such a great sinner against God! What shall I do?' I took him by the hand, and we sat down. He poured out the deep and pent up feelings of his heart; spoke of all his privileges, so many and great—of his dear sister—how earnestly she had desired his salvation. This feeling was the one uppermost. 'Oh, I have been such a great sinner against God, I wonder that I am alive!' We knelt and prayed. He uttered a few broken petitions, but a sense of his deep and dreadful guilt seemed to overwhelm him, and all that I could say or do seemed only to enhance a sense of this. That evening, at his request, I wrote to his father, stating his case. He could not study, and his tutor gave him his option, as to attending recitations. Nothing diverted his attention or had any power to interest him. I never saw a more clear case of the work of the Holy Spirit, giving deep conviction of sin, and of the need of an all-sufficient Saviour.

"At the close of the week I met him, and saw that the deep, settled anxiety he had worn, had given place to a cheerful, tender joy and peace. I asked him, 'Have you found the Saviour?' His answer was, 'I believe I have.'

"There was no ecstasy, no undue excitement,

but a solemn and even cheerful determination to give up all, and, as a lost sinner, to trust in the promise of Christ.

"And so he went on. We often talked and prayed together, and it was a joy and comfort greater than I can express to see the confident faith of that sainted sister realized.

"My memory is stored with many other things, of great interest to me. As you know, we made a tour to Williamstown, Pittsfield, and other places, in September, 1849, and he revelled on the fine scenery during the journey, and both of us enjoyed it exceedingly. Every night and morning we began and ended the day with prayer." * * *

On the first Sabbath in July, 1848, he united with his father's church in Hartford. During the solemn transaction, something occurred, which in other circumstances would have annoyed him greatly. His mother expressed her regret for this. His reply was, "I did not notice it, I was alone with God, entering into solemn covenant with him."

His college life must be passed over briefly, the monotony of which was interrupted by very few incidents.

His summer vacations were spent, either at the sea side, or among the mountains in Berkshire. Here, with a few choice friends, he luxuriated, amid the exuberance of nature's wildest and grandest scenery; and here he gained strength and vigor of mind and body, for the succeeding college campaign. His winter vacations were spent at home.

While in college, he entered the Sabbath school as a teacher, and performed with interest and fidelity his duties, as such.

He also indulged in his favorite musical entertainments, by joining the Beethoven society, and in rendering important assistance in the college choir.

Some of his experience in the course he took in regard to the various college societies may not be deemed out of place here.

Of two of the more important of these, he was a member, the Brothers and the Phi

Beta; but he never joined a secret society. His objections to these were: 1st. They were secret. Everything worth having, would bear to be known. 2d. They were not approved by his parents and judicious friends. 3d. The officers of college were not in favor of them. Then there were certain things connected with them, unfavorable to study; such as late hours, suppers, to say nothing of expenses which the wealthy could meet, but which must be shared equally by all, and for which he felt he had no right to draw upon the resources of his father.

In conversing on the subject after leaving college, he expressed the opinion that he should doubtless have stood better with his classmates, if he had joined them, but that his conscience did not accuse him of having done wrong in the matter.

In 1851, he graduated with no discredit to himself or his college.

It was now an important question, not only to himself but to his parents, how he should put to the right use, qualifications on which so much labor and expense had been bestowed.

During a period of religious interest in college, he had unhesitatingly chosen the ministry as his profession. With this ultimately in view, he decided on spending a year in teaching.

In the autumn of 1851, he entered the high school in his native city, then under the superintendence of Mr. T. Curtis, and remained in connection with it as assistant teacher, for one year. This was a very profitable year to him. Aside from the advantages to be derived from his connection with the school, he had the companionship of Mr. W. B. Capron, then principal of the classical department, now missionary of the American Board in Madura; also a large circle of intelligent Christian friends in the city. In addition to this, his home privileges were not small.

During this year, there was a season of much religious interest in the city. At its close it was apparent to all, that he had been set forward in his Christian course.

CHAPTER V.

THEOLOGICAL STUDIES — CONFLICT — LICENSE — GRADUATES AT ANDOVER — ENTERS ON A FOURTH YEAR AT NEW HAVEN.

In the autumn of 1852, he entered the Theological Seminary at Andover. Before entering, he had been greatly tried in his mind as to his qualifications for the ministry. As months rolled away, his anxiety and perplexity on the subject increased to such a degree as almost to disqualify him for profitable study; and he came at length to doubt, whether he was in reality a Christian. Twice during his second year, he came home with the intention of laying open his case to his father; but he was prostrated by severe illness, and he could not add to his trouble. They were indeed deep waters, through which he was then passing. It was evident to those who best knew him, that something was weighing heavily on his spirit. He was not buoyant and cheerful as formerly; but it was only to his mother that his feelings were disclosed. These were months of trial, to both mother and son. It was her prevailing hope that God was thus leading him as it were through the fires, that he might purify him from the dross of selfishness, pride, and ambition, and that he would one day bring him forth, a workman meet for the master's service. His health suffered; an impenetrable cloud rested on the pathway before him. He could not go forward in his preparation for the ministry. At length as the vacation at the end of the year drew near its close, and he must return to Andover if he returned at all, and enter upon his third year, he made a full disclosure to his father. This was, as he supposed it must be, an unexpected and severe trial to him. His father could not advise him to go forward and enter the ministry in the state of feeling in which he then was; but thought he should return to Andover, and continue his studies, and wait the indications of Providence in this matter. In the meantime, he advised him to see Professor Barrows, and lay open his case to him. Professor Barrows has kindly furnished the writer with an account of what he styles, "that mental conflict which constituted the crisis of his life after he began his theological studies:"

"My first acquaintance with the late Rev. Erskine J. Hawes, was in Andover Theological Seminary, where I knew him as a modest, pure minded, earnest, and studious young man, who gave good promise of future usefulness in the gospel ministry. As he advanced in the theological course, a tinge of despondency began to manifest itself in his conversation and general demeanor. I witnessed this with some uneasiness, fearing that he might settle down into an unhealthy tone of feeling, which would weaken his interest in his studies, and impair the thoroughness of his preparation for the ministerial work. A letter received about this time from his father who had not failed to notice the depression of his spirits in view of the ministerial office for which he was preparing himself, increased my solicitude in his behalf. As I was inquiring with myself how I might approach him on the subject without repelling him by apparent obtrusiveness, he relieved me of my embarrassment by seeking an interview with me.

"He began by saying, as nearly as I can remember his words: 'I have about made up my mind to renounce the work of preparation for the ministry. I do not think that I have the qualifications necessary to make me an efficient preacher of the Gospel; and the idea of being a poor preacher, an incumbrance to the sacred office, is what I cannot bear.' My first effort was to induce him to suspend his decision, and this point I argued very earnestly with him, urging him to do nothing rashly, and endeavoring to show him that, even should he not enter the ministry, the course of theological training to which he was subjecting himself would abundantly repay the labor bestowed upon it. But he continued to repeat, in various forms, the difficulty with which he had opened the interview. In doing so he was very modest and respectful, for it did not belong to either his nature or his education to be otherwise; but at the same time he was very earnest and persevering. 'You would not advise,' he said, 'that all should be min-sisters of the Gospel. One man can do most good in the ministry because he has the requisite qualifications for it. Another can do more good in some other calling. To urge him forward would be no favor to him or to the churches.' That there are men in the sacred office who are an incumbrance to it, and who would relieve the churches by demitting it, seemed to rest heavily on his spirits, and he more than once adverted to the fact, repeating the declaration: 'I do not wish to be such a minister.' Of course I could not deny the premises from which he argued. I frankly admitted the facts; and added, if I rightly recollect, that I believed in both the good judgment and candor of his friends, who had advised him to seek the sacred office, because they judged that he had the requisite qualifications for it. Yet it did not seem to me that I succeeded in making much impression upon his mind.

"At this distance of time I am not able to say whether it was at a later stage of the interview just related, or during another and subsequent interview, that I turned the discussion into a different channel, and as I had reason to believe, with much better success. With regard to his objection of wanting the proper qualifications for a gospel minister, I told him that if he meant qualifications to occupy a high station in the church, as the world counts highness, the sooner he laid aside that idea, the better; since the young man who seeks the sacred office with such a thought before his mind is sure to be corrupted by the bad leaven of worldly ambition. I dwelt at some length on the fact that it is only a few of Christ's servants on whom he bestows the good gift of commanding eloquence and influence; that the idea that only such men should be preachers of the Gospel is simply absurd; that the true question to be settled by a young man and his friends, should be whether there is reasonable ground for believing that he can serve Christ acceptably in the ministry in some position, though it be not among those which the world calls high: that he who has a right view of the ministerial office will seek it purely from its spiritual attractions, because he loves and covets the work itself of guiding sinners to Christ, and building up Christ's disciples in the faith; and that such a spirit will prepare him to labor cheerfully and contentedly in any post to which the providence of God may call him, though it be among those that the world calls obscure, where often the most real good is accomplished; that, if the master should have need for him in a station of commanding influence, he will signify it at the proper time; if not, no harm is done. I told him further that I was not sorry to witness in him this mental conflict, for I believed that by it the Spirit of God was prèparing him to be a preacher of the Gospel in deed and in truth; that it is God's way to put those whom he is preparing for true usefulness into the fire, either before their entrance upon the sacred office, or afterwards; that thus their self-reliance and worldly views may be burnt out of them, and they may learn to lean implicitly upon his grace, and seek simply his glory.

"To this presentation of the spiritual side of the ministerial office he listened with earnest silence, without making, so far as I can now remember, any reply, except to thank me for the interest I had manifested in his case. How much impression it made upon him, I cannot say. I thought at the time, that, along with the influences that were operating upon him from other sources, the Spirit of God was pleased to make some use of it to guide him to a right decision of the momentous question before him. However this may have been, he came to me a few days afterwards, with a countenance illuminated by the holy composure that had taken possession of his soul, and said: 'Well, I have determined to go on, and do the best I can.' From that time, I never witnessed any wavering in his purpose. This decision, made, as I fully believe, under the influence of the Holy Spirit, seemed to impart new life and energy to him, intellectually as well as morally. His friends noticed with pleasure the new interest with which he viewed the whole field of theological inquiry. He looked upon the doctrines of the Gospel from the spiritual side, and entered upon the investigation of them, not only as a matter of intellectual pastime, but as one who believed them to be 'the panoply of God,' wherewith he arms his ministers, that they may wage a successful war against the world, the flesh, and the devil—a panoply which he hoped to be permitted soon to put on, that in it he might himself fight the good fight of faith.

"After he left the seminary I followed his

movements with deep interest, and learned with great pleasure of his settlement among a united people, who loved him, and whom he loved in return; among whom he devoted himself, so earnestly and successfully, to the great work of preaching Christ crucified. To human view, he had the prospect of a long and faithful ministry. But it was God's purpose that it should be—how brief! When the news that it had in very deed closed forever, first reached us here, it was so astounding that we could hardly believe it. But we remembered that God has done the same thing before, in a much higher sphere than any of us are permitted to occupy. How full of wonderful meaning is that simple sentence of holy writ: 'And he killed James, the brother of John, with the sword.' James had been three years under our Lord's personal training. He was one of the three favored apostles whom he admitted to peculiar intimacy with himself; who alone were permitted to witness the raising of Jairus's daughter, the transfiguration, and the agony in Gethsemane. Yet, after a ministry of only a few years, he who had all power in heaven and earth, suffered James to perish by the sword of Herod. He did not esteem his ministry too brief for all the divine culture which he had himself bestowed upon him, much less should we have any such reasonings in respect to the human culture bestowed upon our departed friend. In carrying forward his cause, our heavenly Master is never straitened for resources. He cares not so much for the quantity of our labor as its quality. He wants the whole heart, and then he will accept it, and order by his own unerring wisdom the limits of our earthly service.

E. BARROWS.

Andover Theol. Sem., Nov. 30, 1860.

After these interviews with Dr. Barrows, he proceeded with more comfort to himself, and also more successfully in his preparation for the work of the ministry.

He was examined and licensed, Jan. 15th,

1855, by the Fourth Association of Hartford County, assembled in his father's study.

He graduated at the Theological Seminary, Andover, August, 1855; and entered upon a fourth year at New Haven, in the month of October following.

This was a broken year, much of it was devoted to the improvement of his health. But although unable to study much, he yet performed a good degree of pulpit service, both in his own and a neighboring state. During this year, he had some favorable opportunities for settlement; but his estimate of the sacred office, the high standard he had set for himself as a suitable qualification for the work of the ministry, made him shrink back for a time, from taking upon himself its responsibilities and duties. The state of his health also had some weight in the matter.

CHAPTER VI.

CALL TO GREENFIELD — PREACHES AT FALMOUTH—WESTERN TOUR.

In the month of May, 1856, he was invited to preach at Greenfield, Mass. He accepted the invitation, and was there three Sabbaths. The result of his preaching there has been kindly furnished by one of the prominent members of the church, the Honorable Judge Grinnell.

In a letter of sympathy to the bereaved parents, he writes:

"My acquaintance with your son, brief as it was, was tenderly interesting, and at one time I hoped it would be lasting. * * * His preaching, his social, Christian and ministerial deportment, won the love and respect of our people. His sermons were faithful and earnest exhibitions of Christian truth and duty. I well remember the impressions made upon me and others by this lovely young teacher. A general and strong desire was felt to extend to him an invitation to settle with us in the ministry; and a vote was given with great unanimity by both the church and society in favor of such invitation. An annual salary of $1,000 was offered,—a greater sum than the society had ever before paid their minister.

"Mr. Hawes took the matter of this call into deliberate consideration, as a man of honorable and conscientious character would surely do. He declined a settlement, assigning, as one reason, a doubt whether the then state of his health would admit of his assuming the labors and responsibilities of the pastorate over this church and people.

"The decision could not but be painful to us."

The decision of this question cost the youthful candidate much serious and anxious inquiry, and many sleepless nights were passed before he could come to any satisfactory result as to his duty, either in declining or accepting the call. The unanimity of the call seemed clearly to point to the duty of his acceptance. The conditions appended, and the compensation, were every way satisfactory—the place to him had attractions as a residence—the society was refined and intelligent, and he already felt a very tender friendship for several of the elder and influential members of the church.

The people had given him evidence of their satisfaction with his preaching, and in respect to this part of his labors he had reason to hope that he should not disappoint them. But, would his health endure the pressure that must be brought to bear upon it, in the efforts necessary to maintain the general interests of the church and congregation? Of these he had taken no superficial view, and this turned the balance on the negative side.

His answer, declining an acceptance of the call, bears date June 15th, 1856. In reviewing his decision afterwards, he felt that he had acted wisely, as he had conscientiously; his health would not have endured the trial.

During the summer and autumn following, he was constantly engaged in supplying vacant pulpits, except during a few weeks, when he was confined at home by severe illness.

In December, 1856, he was induced to take charge of the congregation of the Rev. Dr. Hooker, of Falmouth, who was obliged to take his wife abroad on account of ill-health.

In regard to the labors of the pastor whose church he had taken in charge for a few months, he writes: "I find that Dr. Hooker has been in the habit of conducting most of his meetings himself, walking to the different districts where the meetings were to be held, and back again, as a general thing. There are three districts which he visits in this way. He told me that he had not failed of an appointment once on account of ill-health during the twenty past years of his ministry,—out, rain or shine, walking two or three miles to lecture, and back in the evening." "I shall be obliged to work exceedingly hard to tread in his footsteps."

Of his first Sabbath, he writes: "I preached yesterday to a very attentive and respectable audience, and took charge in the evening of the Sunday-school concert. I believe it was the first time I ever attempted to address children; and though I think what I said could not be very interesting or edifying to grown-up persons, and was not free from blunders and inelegancies, still I seemed to have the attention of the young, and hope that they were both interested and profited."

On entering upon his pulpit labors in Falmouth, he kept the principle which he had adopted when first he commenced making sermons, steadily in view, viz., the profit of the hearers. To qualify himself the better for this, he commenced a systematic course of Scripture reading. He writes: "I am studying Romans in course, with such helps as I can command in an old Greek Testament and Lexicon, but with the serviceable aid, however, of Stewart, Barnes and Chalmers. I can never read the latter without being profited highly, in having my own mind quickened, and made bolder and prepared to encounter difficulties. Besides this, he is eminently suggestive. The more I study, the more I am ashamed of my ignorance of the Scriptures. In writing my sermons, I find myself often obliged to stop and go to investigating more closely."

Again he writes: "Since I have commenced lecturing, in connection with my other duties, I have been obliged to lay aside my exegetical study and doctrinal reading, except so far as is connected with my preparation for the pulpit and lecture-room. I must return to these again. I have been spending upon my own resources too much,—have been giving myself too exclusively to the preparation for the pulpit and too little to the study of, and the storing my mind with, such truths as shall refresh and quicken the sensibilities, and keep me lively and earnest in the great matters of religion."

From the commencement of his labors in Falmouth, he had a very ardent desire to see a revival of religion among the people. He was strengthened in his efforts for this by a similar desire on the part of the absent pastor.

He writes: "I am encouraged by his prayers and good wishes that my labors may be blessed in his absence;—and I find, also, this to be the general desire and hope. May it be realized!"

"I often find myself casting my thoughts forward, and wondering how, with my limited experience, I should succeed in conducting a revival if the Lord should see fit to bless my labors. * * * My sermons I have made as direct as possible, and as close to the conscience; but the residue of the spirit is with the Lord. Now and then, I hear of one and another, made serious by this or that discourse; but there has been so much interruption to the meetings this winter, and there is so much to divert the attention as the spring comes on, that my faith is somewhat shaken. Much of the interruption to the meetings during the winter was owing to the weather." He writes: "The oldest inhabitants do not remember such a winter for severity. The snow was, at one time, banked up in places eight or ten feet high, the roads impassable, and for a week there was no mail." Again, in February, he writes: "A multitude of unpleasant Sabbaths. They tell me I have not yet seen my entire congregation together. The weather is now milder; the snow is disappearing again as fast as it came; it melts away like magic under the mild, soft breezes from the sea."

The diversion of which he spoke as the spring approached, was from another and a more absorbing object. The people were about remodeling their old church.

March 4th, he writes: "The first of April we leave the old church. I am preparing a sermon for the occasion; shall take for my text: 'If I forget thee, O Jerusalem,' etc., confining my remarks, not so much to the propriety of beautifying places of worship as to 'appropriate reflections on leaving an old sanctuary.'" The following is a brief abstract of portions of the sermon:

"The purpose of the captive exile, 'to remember, and not forget Jerusalem,' as he 'wept by the rivers of Babylon,'" although uttered in circumstances so unlike those of the worshippers in that old sanctuary about to be taken down, yet furnished a model sufficiently suggestive of thoughts for the illustration of the subject.

"Associations that cluster in memory around the place of one's birth,—tender recollections of childhood and of home,—the chamber where was lisped the first prayer of infancy,—the family altar, with all its hallowed remembrances."—Scenes, such as these, were happily introduced to illustrate the more sacred and endearing associations that cluster around an old sanctuary, the place of one's spiritual birth.

"The Theophanies in the ancient Temple, accompanying the gorgeous rites and imposing ceremonies of Jewish worship," were introduced, "to show in strong contrast the superiority of those manifestations with which the great Head of the Church now condescends to bless his true worshippers, in his spiritual sanctuary, of which the ancient temple worship was but the shadow:—with such seasons of divine manifestation, the memory of this sanctuary will be associated in after years." Such were some of the thoughts presented in the commencement of the sermon—the last ever preached in that old church, the spiritual birthplace of many of its aged, as also of its youthful worshippers.

When about to leave Falmouth, he suffered much in thought of the unfruitfulness of his ministry there;—lamented that he must leave the people as he found them. He had endeavored to preach the pure Gospel, was not conscious of having spared himself in case of any duty or labor, yet he saw no saving results. This, he thought, must be owing to some defect in his ministry.

He says: "All are very attentive, and from some hints I have occasionally received, I believe my preaching is very well liked; but this is speaking too favorably of myself. Last Sabbath, in the afternoon, *I felt myself dreadfully deserted.* I was so ashamed that I did not once look at the audience."

It should be recorded with gratitude here, that he was not always left thus. After his settlement in the ministry, he said to a friend: "I sometimes go into my lecture-room, feeling sadly depressed, but the Lord wonderfully sustains me."

It seems due to the youthful preacher to state a fact here, touching the acceptableness of his ministerial labors in Falmouth. The people had some reason to suppose that they should at no distant day be deprived of the labors of their much-loved and respected pastor. And such proved to be the fact. Before formally announcing to his people his intention of leaving them, the Rev. Dr. Hooker communicated with the subject of this memoir, assuring him, that in case he left, the people of Falmouth would look to him to fill the vacancy. But for reasons which appeared satisfactory to himself, and also to his father, he discouraged any such expectation on their part.

Before leaving Falmouth, in a letter to his father, he says: "There is one plan on which my mind has dwelt much of late. I have not mentioned it to you, except casually: it is the idea of travelling. It seems to me that it is just the experience that I need. I feel an irrepressible desire to visit the East. I merely mention the matter to know what you think of it."

This desire was gradually ripening into a purpose after his settlement in the ministry. The idea of one day "standing by his sister's grave," was looked forward to, as more than a possible event.

But another and a speedier meeting had been arranged for him, not on Moslem soil, surrounded by the gloomy receptacles of the dead, but, as there is every reason to believe, amid the splendors of a heavenly home,—not to weep over the silent dust, from which could come no response or note of recognition, but to be actually in the presence of her, who, "having gone before, was waiting to welcome him to the joys of pure and delightful fellowship in the courts above."*

Just before his return home, his father wrote to secure his services for one Sabbath. He wrote in answer, "I must say that I look forward with some trepidation to supplying our pulpit, for I am inclined to regard the sermons which I have prepared as better adapted to some other people than to the great and the wise of our congregation. Indeed, I wonder, when I think with how little fear I made my first appearance in our pulpit, with my meager modicum of truth with which to feed those of vastly larger experience than myself. And it is when reviewing these first efforts that I find my confidence shaken at the thought of again appearing before our people. It seems to me as if I was made growingly sensible of my imperfections. I wish some other arrangement could be made. Perhaps, H—— would like to exchange." That exchange was made.

* Extract from his sermon, preached on occasion of leaving the old church at Falmouth.

On the return of Dr. Hooker to his charge in Falmouth, Erskine returned to his home in Hartford, and began maturing a plan of travel. In consequence of a letter from La Crosse, Wisconsin, he decided on going West, not that he had any expectation of settling there, but the letter was made the occasion of visiting that part of the country. Before leaving home, among other places, he preached one Sabbath in Plymouth, Ct. This was the last Sabbath in May, 1857. His going there, as it appeared at the time, was merely accidental. Another person had engaged to supply the pulpit, but being unable, for some reason, to do it, he requested E. to go in his place. He went and preached, returned home, and thought no more of it. Not so the Plymouth people.

In the month of June, 1857, he started on his western tour. Having never been further in that direction than the falls of Niagara, everything to him was, of course, new and strange. His vivid descriptions in his letters home, furnish a rich dioramic view of the

States through which he passed. At St. Louis, where he spent several days, and where, through the kindness of friends residing there, he had been shown something of the "magnitude and extent of the immense business" carried on in that "*world of itself*," not forgetting to mention "one of the finest sermons ever heard in his life," to which it was his privilege to listen during the Sabbath spent there,—at St. Louis, he "embarked, for the first time," on the bosom of the great "Father of Waters."

One reason for his making this tour was, to ascertain his qualifications, or rather disqualifications, for a settlement at the West. With this object steadily in view, he looked at the country, its scenery, its resources, its inhabitants, its pulpits, and its preachers.

The vast outlay in public works, the magnificence of public buildings, most of which were in an unfinished state, but all indicating the "activity and thrift of an enterprising people" were very astonishing to a staid, cautious, eastern mind like his. While everything was "yet in embryo" and "*intensely new*, the people were pushing matters as though large cities were actually theirs in possession."

In regard to the "natural scenery of the country," he was "sure that the long, unbroken, verdant prairies, so beautiful to some, would, in time, become wearisome to his eye, which had been educated to love mountain scenery."

As to the pulpit, he was quite sure "he should not suit a western audience." They demanded a more direct *ad hominem* mode of address than pervaded his written discourses.

At St. Anthony, where the river, "hemmed in between its broken and precipitous banks, furnishes an agreeable contrast to the uninteresting level everywhere around," he turned his face homeward.

"Up to this time," he writes home, that "he has never yet seen the place where he could say he was a stranger in a strange land," but everywhere he had found friends, who had contributed to render his visit not only agreeable but profitable. Even here, at this furthest point, he was "greatly cheered" by finding a classmate, whom he highly respected, "the last one who, he should suppose, could accommodate himself to the *rough and tumble* of western life," settled down to the practice of the law.

On his return, he stopped at different points on the river, and took a different route on his way home.

Among other important objects gained by this journey, he gained this,—a settled conviction that New England was the place for him; that his education, his tastes, his habits, all required the surroundings of New England society, to enable him to pass life, not only agreeably but usefully, and he "had returned," as he said, "quite willing to settle down in a New England pulpit."

CHAPTER VII.

CALL AND SETTLEMENT AT PLYMOUTH—LETTERS HOME DURING A PERIOD OF RELIGIOUS INTEREST AMONG HIS PEOPLE.

It has been stated, that before leaving home, he preached one Sabbath in Plymouth, then destitute of a pastor. Immediately on his return, he was invited to preach as a candidate with reference to a settlement there. This he declined, but consented to preach a few Sabbaths as a supply. In the mean time, he was balancing the question in his own mind of a settlement in one of two or three other places, which had opened favorably before him, and where, by encouraging a movement, he might doubtless be eligibly located. But before any decided action had been taken in either case, a call came from the Plymouth people under such circumstances that he could not choose but listen to it. The indications of Providence were so manifest as to leave him scarcely any option in the case.

His answer accepting the call bears date December 5th, 1857. Having decided on a place of settlement, he set himself to a careful preparation for the performance of his labors in that part of the vineyard, which seemed to be the will of his Master that he should cultivate. This work he carried forward with great seriousness.

His first inquiry respected his own personal religion. His self-examination was deep and thorough. The chamber where he had been taught to lisp the first prayer of infancy, now became the place of deep heart-searchings, and earnest supplications, for divine light and guidance.

He next reviewed the great and fundamental doctrines of the Gospel. These he took up one by one, and having examined each carefully and prayerfully, formed them into a digest of religious belief, and adopted this as his creed to present before the council at his examination.

The time intervening between his acceptance of the call and settlement, was a very profitable season to him. Favored beyond most young men who are looking forward to the ministry in having the wise and judicious instruction, and counsel, of a father who had been long a faithful and successful preacher of the Gospel, surrounded by intelligent Christian friends, and a home furnished with all the means requisite to the formation of the Christian as well as of the ministerial character, and having with all a mind that could appreciate these privileges, he could not but be well qualified for his work.

With customary forethought, he provided for himself a home among the people of his future charge. His study was preëminently his home. In securing this he was very happy. The house in which it was located, having been the residence of a loved and venerated pastor, who was sleeping at no great distance among the people of his charge, the monumental stone being visible, in passing to and from the church where he ministered, serving to awaken associations of the most hallowed and profitable kind. On a mind like his, which regarded nothing as unimportant that could be made, though in a small degree, to contribute to the successful prosecution of the ministerial work, they were not lost.

His introductory sermon was also in readiness, so that when the important hour arrived, the hour, to him, only second in solemnity to the last tribunal, he had nothing to do but to present himself before the council for examination.

With great self-possession, and with real modesty of mien and manner, the youthful candidate sustained a strict and somewhat protracted examination, standing for full three hours, and answering without note the questions usually asked on such occasions; showing by the readiness and pertinence of his answers that he had made no superficial preparation for that hour of trial,—and more than this, that he regarded the office of the ministry as a high and sacred calling, involving responsibilities of no ordinary nature,—responsibilities to be met and accounted for in another place, and before another tribunal than the one then and there gathered.

The ordination services were on the day following, January 19th, 1858. As there are no printed documents to refer to, these must be passed over in silence, with the simple notice that the sermon was by the father of the youthful candidate, and was listened to, with tender interest by one hearer at least.

On the afternoon after his ordination, having received the calls and congratulations of several of the leading people of his congregation, he took his father round and called on some who were ill and could not attend the services, thus early manifesting his interest in every individual of his new charge. It is pleasant to reflect, that this interest suffered no abatement but steadily increased during the period of his brief ministry.

A few sketches from his letters home will serve to illustrate the spirit and temper with which he entered upon and performed the new and varied duties of his ministerial work.

To his mother: "January 22d, 1858. Well! the excitement of ordination is over, and I have now fairly entered on the arduous and responsible duties of a settled minister. May God give me wisdom and grace to meet them calmly as they come, and to discharge them in humble dependence on Him for his aid. * * * * After the fatigue and excitement of the week, I do not feel much like doing any great things. I am heartily glad that my introductory sermons are all prepared for the Sabbath. If they were not, I might be thrown into a sad state of trepidation, which would be very disastrous at the outset of my ministry. * * *

February 9th, 1858. To his mother: "You may have been surprised at not seeing me on Monday as you expected, but now that I have a parish to look after, you must expect to have a great many such surprises. I had a funeral to attend yesterday, which necessarily kept me at home; and as I am now exceedingly busy in making the acquaintance of my parishioners, and am expecting to have another funeral to attend soon, I cannot tell when you will see me. I find that the parish is much more scattered than I supposed, but after I have gone the rounds, and become better acquainted with the localities, then the labor will be rendered easier by systematizing matters. I have a prayer-meeting to attend on Thursday evening, and have started again the Sabbath-school concert, which has not been regularly held, as such, for a long time. I mean that the Sabbath-school shall have my first attention, and also the monthly concert for missions."

"February 12th, 1858. * * * I rejoice to hear, both from you and the religious papers, that there is so much interest in Hartford, and especially among the young. I hope it may increase. I wish we might see some signs of awakening here. It seems to me very desirable now at the commencement of my ministry. My prayer is, that I may not stand in the way of such a work, and that the Lord would give me more of a revival spirit than I already possess, and qualify me for such a service. There is interest all up and down the Naugatuck valley, and on either side of us.

"I am preparing a sermon for the Sabbath on the text: 'They that be wise shall shine as the light,' etc. Subject: Incentives which should lead professing Christians to put forth personal and earnest efforts for the salvation of their fellow men. May the Spirit make it effectual in the awakening of Christians in this place to the state of the impenitent around them." * * *

"February 18th, 1858. * * * I hope my mind may become less encumbered with the duties of my parish. But I must confess that I have yet to learn the art of throwing off care at the proper time, and taking things as they come. I am always inclined to anticipate duty, and there is indeed something comfortable in being able to survey a duty in the distance, and as it approaches think that you are all prepared to meet it. * * *

"I am writing a sermon on the text: 'Restore unto me the joy of thy salvation,' etc. I hope to be able to bring it before the people on the coming Sabbath, as it contains a subject which seems peculiarly adapted to the present state of things in the church. In a note which I wrote this evening to one of the brethren, I suggested the following plan, which I presume they are discussing at the meeting, viz.: to have a Committee appointed to call on the different members of the church and ascertain what is the state of religion, both with themselves and in their families. I hope the plan may gain their approval and be productive of good." * * *

"March 7th, 1858. * * * Sunday-school concert this evening—very fully attended. The Committee, who were appointed to visit the different families, went their rounds and gave in very interesting reports, last Wednesday afternoon. Some cases of inquiry have come to light, and I have appointed Tuesday evening to see any individuals who may wish to converse on the subject of religion. The appearance of things is encouraging. Some have already come out and expressed a hope in Christ." * * *

"March 23d, 1858. * * * I wish that I could be present and attend some of the religious meetings of which I hear such interesting accounts, and I have had serious thoughts of doing so, but have about given them up, at least for the present, because I have so much to attend to. Though there is as yet here no very wide-spread interest, still there are a few cases of inquiry, and the state of things seems to demand an increase of meetings. I appointed Monday evening to see any who might wish to inquire, and at the same time the brethren held a meeting in the vestry. There were some six or seven who called on me for religious conversation. I have had three such meetings, and about the same number each evening. The signs, I think, are encouraging. I feel more than ever the need of divine aid in all my services, and especially when directing others in the way of eternal life. I have been more fully persuaded than ever, of late, of the utter inefficiency of means without the aid of God's spirit, and have endeavored to throw myself more entirely on the divine sovereignty, on which I love to dwell in my thoughts. * * *

"The preparation of a sermon for fast-day, as well as for the coming Sabbath, aside from the other services, will keep me very busy. It has been thought best to appoint a meeting of some kind on Sabbath evening, in order to deepen any impression which may have been made during the day. The young men have started a Wednesday evening prayer-meeting—meeting for conference and prayer on Thursday evening. There is also a female prayer-meeting during the week." * * *

"April 6th, 1858. My dear Father: It was my intention to have spent two or three days of this week at home, for the purpose of attending the religious services in the city. I have no doubt it would have been every way profitable to me as I need a change. As the interest, however, is deepening among my own people, I feel that I cannot leave judiciously, but must stay by to direct and counsel. I have appointed Monday evening to see inquirers. Last evening there were some fourteen in my room, some of whom were under very deep conviction. There have been some conversions,—one of a young man, who has been considered a very hopeless case. But there is one thing that distresses me,—the church are not awake and active as they should be. Some few are taking a noble stand, and are a real help; but the majority do not seem to realize the fact, that the Spirit of the Lord is at work on the hearts of the impenitent, and that all they have to do is to put in the sickle. I am willing to work in my own imperfect way just as the Lord gives me strength, but I cannot do everything. I spent all of Saturday, and a part of yesterday and to-day in calling on those who have been to converse with me on the subject of religion. It taxes the body, but is pleasant to the soul. To-day I feel nearly exhausted, but I desire to lie like an instrument in the hands of God, and it is my earnest prayer that He will serve Himself with me just as He may see fit. Sometimes I think I shall not live very long, and this makes me want to live all the faster. It seems strange to me that the people here do not take hold more in earnest, when there is such encouragement to labor. The impenitent are peculiarly accessible. Yesterday I went up into the north part of the town,—stopped at a house, and had a few moments' conversation with an individual, whom I at once found ready to converse on the subject of religion, and very tender. This is only one of many instances. But I have not time nor strength to do all I would; and I cannot say that I am well, and I greatly desire that the people should do more, both to assist me, and for their own good. Being new in the business, I do not know how many meetings it is wise to have. Our services are these: Sunday evening, prayer-meeting; Monday evening, see inquirers; Wednesday evening, young people's meeting; Thursday evening, conference and prayer. Do you think these are sufficient? There are some cases of inquiry which sorely perplex me: one or two individuals who have been a long time in the dark, and get no light, and nothing I can say to them seems to do them any good. Then, with regard to those who indulge a hope, I am exceedingly afraid to say anything to encourage them, for fear they may be mistaken, what do you do with these? what counsels do you think it best to give to those just commencing a religious life, and what exercises do you think it best to conduct for their particular benefit? So many questions come up that I scarcely know in what order to state them. I feel my exceeding weakness and ignorance, oftentimes, in conversing with and directing inquirers. It is a fearful responsibility. Can you not come out here and spend next Sabbath, or the Sabbath after, and one or two days, by getting a supply for your own pulpit? It would greatly assist me, and awaken the people. It seems to me that if we could have one or two heavy blows struck just at this time, it would be just what we need. You would then, by personal observation, tell me what course you think I had better pursue.

"But I cannot write more. Affectionate regards to mother. Your affectionate son,

"E. J. Hawes."

This urgent request coming from an only and tenderly loved son, the father could not comply with, as he had more than he could possibly do at home, there being an unusual interest among his own people. In his bereaved hopes, the grieved child thus writes:

"April 14th, 1858. My dear Father: I regretted, exceedingly, that you could not find it convenient to be present here on Monday. On the strength of what mother wrote, I appointed a meeting for Monday evening, without stating definitely the form which the exercises would take, but merely mentioning that I expected you to be here and to bear some part in the services. Some doubtless came expecting to see you, and went away disappointed. We, however, had a pleasant, and, I hope, a profitable meeting, but it put an additional burden on me, which I felt hardly able to bear, as duties have increased much of late. On Sunday, besides preaching during the day, I attended a funeral in the afternoon, where I made an address;* then married a couple in church, after which I availed myself of the audience in attendance to dispense the Word once more in their hearing. (The meeting of Monday evening has been mentioned.) Tuesday evening I attended the Young People's meeting. This evening (Wednesday) I have just been seeing inquirers; to-morrow evening I attend the meeting for conference and prayer. Besides, I feel it my duty to look

* The custom of the place required this.

continually after those under concern, by calling on them at their houses. Some one must do the work, or else the interest, what there is, will flag. I could wish that the members of the church were more engaged. I do what I can myself, and, after all, mourn that I can do so little.

"There have been some interesting conversions, which have afforded me much encouragement, but I am annoyed with the fact, that on the minds of some young men who have been interested, there are evil influences brought to bear from without, weakening their serious impressions, and leading them to give up the subject. It is discouraging to see a person one evening seemingly near the kingdom of heaven, and then to call on him a day or two afterwards and find that instead of gaining, he has lost ground, and that, through the influence of some ungodly associate. It is hard to be obliged to work against these counter influences. There have been a few precious drops, but I desire to see a more copious shower like that which has blest a town adjacent. I wish to see you very much for the purpose of talking over matters and things here. I thought if you could only come and give us one or two of your stirring sermons, the effect would be most salutary, but I shall not invite you again. I will only say, that in my weakness such a visit from you at this time would be most acceptable and opportune. It is a wonder to me that all the church are not awake and active when the impenitent seem so ready to be conversed with. But whatever others may do, I shall labor for the Lord just as long as He gives me strength. I have come to the resolution to find out just how every one stands on the subject of religion, who is in the habit of attending my church, and at least let him know that I feel deeply for his salvation."

In justice to the father, it should be stated here, that however grateful it would have been to him to have aided his son, yet that his own labors were so varied and increased by an unusual interest in his own parish, it was impossible for him to do so.

"April 20th, 1858. My dear Mother: I cannot forbear writing a line to you before retiring. The Spirit of the Lord, I believe, is present with us in power. This evening I went into the young people's meeting, and was at once awed at the solemnity which was manifest. It has been my custom to run in just before the close of this meeting, and make a few remarks, concluding with a brief prayer. Judge of my surprise when one, and then another of those who had been known to be impenitent arose, and in a few, simple, direct words declared their purpose to live for Christ. Some of these had previously conversed with me on the subject of religion, others had not. Five of these are remarkable conversions; young men, who, perhaps, have been regarded as far from the right way as any in P——. One of these was in my room last evening, and I shall never forget the look which he gave me when I asked him how he felt, and his reply:

"I have had for the last week just religion enough to make me most dreadfully wretched." But this evening he is calm and peaceful. Prayer-meetings are being multiplied,—several being held the same evening in different neighborhoods. I wish I could attend them all, but this of course is impossible.

"Christians are beginning to awake. Mr. —— is really roused, and being a man of influence, gives me most essential aid. His wife, also, is a most efficient helper. She is new in the divine life. He has passed through a new conversion of late, and is constantly going round among the impenitent and laboring with them. He is a man whom all love and esteem, and who has, perhaps, a greater influence over all classes than any other man in P——.

"This is a glorious state of things for this church, for its tendency will be to cement the brethren still more closely in the bonds of love. In the course of my pastoral visits, and I have done a good deal of *that* of late, I am continually meeting with those who are tender on the subject of religion. It is interesting to ask the question of an individual, how the matter stands with his soul? and to find that the Lord has already gone before you, and been at work on that soul by his Spirit. Many such cases have come to my notice in different parts of the town. Some have come to me, whom I have never seen or heard of before, and of course did not know to be interested, and have declared their faith in Christ. The matter has been simply between them and Christ, with their Bible as their guide. But I cannot write more, though I have much to write. I said this evening I would give a great deal if father would run down here, just at this time, and give me a week's assistance and counsel, for I do not know how I am going to meet all the labor which is to be devolved upon me. I do not know what to do. It is pleasant to visit and very necessary, but then it takes up my time, and I find it somewhat dissipating to thought. Of course I have no time for reading or study, and this alarms me. I am exceedingly afraid, with the constant draughts made on me, I shall run dry.

"Remember me in your prayers that my strength fail not. I feel it a very solemn responsibility to attempt the guidance of souls. I feel my utter impotency, and after I have been seeing inquirers, feel sorely distressed and dissatisfied with myself that I have done so poorly in pointing them to a Saviour. Many cases perplex me exceedingly."

We will leave him here in the midst of this period of religious interest, with simply remarking, that he probably had less cause than usually falls to the lot of many pastors at the close of a revival like that with which his people were blest, to lament over those, who, having begun the Christian course, turned back again to the world, and thus gave evidence that they never were truly converted.

His letters home during the two succeeding years of his ministry, furnish ample evidence of his tender, faithful watch and care of those "over whom the Holy Ghost had made him overseer," that he "might present them," "*every one of them*," "faultless before the throne, in that day," when their souls should be required at his hand.

He lived only for his people,—he labored only for them. Their temporal as well as their spiritual good lay near his heart. In all their plans for the improvement of morals in the place, he rendered very efficient aid, both by his wise counsels and judicious efforts. Especially was this true in the cause of temperance, in which he took a prominent part. At the time of his death, he was interested in a plan for the improvement of the grounds around his church,—and much more deeply interested in what at all times lay near his heart, but now pressed with unusual weight upon it, the reviving of the interest in religion, which had begun sadly to decline among his own people.* During the winter following the revival among his people, a certain amusement had been

* See a notice of this in the article by his friend Monteith.

introduced which had a direct tendency to draw off the attention of the young from serious things. In this amusement, he learned with pain, that two of the younger members of his church had been drawn in to participate. Wishing to prepare a sermon to meet the case, he sent home for the best tracts on the subject. The tracts were sent, and with them this short piece of advice from his father: "'Never take a horse by the hind foot while he is eating his oats.' Wait till the excitement is over, and then it will do for you to preach on the subject." This judicious advice was acted upon, and thus much exciting and unprofitable discussion on the subject of dancing was avoided, which would have been unhappy at the time, as there was still some lingering seriousness in the place.

CHAPTER VIII.

BRIEF NOTICES OF HIS MINISTRY BY OTHERS—CHARACTERISTICS—HIS PREACHING.

When it was in contemplation to prepare something that might serve as a remembrancer of what he was, and of what he did, a request was made to his people in Plymouth to furnish such items of interest in his ministry among them, as they might wish to have preserved for their own use, and also for the little ones of his parish, who were too young to appreciate his labors for their good, when he was taken from them.

A few such items have been kindly furnished. The first is from the youngest member in his church—spoken of as the "lamb in his flock." It will serve as a specimen of the course he took with those converted under his ministry.

* * "Some of us remember him as the

best friend we ever had. His words first led us to see our own sinfulness in the sight of a Holy God, and to cry out '*what must we do to be saved?*' Then, he pointed us to the '*Lamb of God, that taketh away the sins of the world,*' and gently has he led us on ever since,—reproving us when he saw us going wrong, and encouraging us to press onward in the straight and narrow way."

A loved member of his church, a subject of the revival, thus writes:

"When the Rev. E. J. Hawes was sent to watch over us, we had been for nearly two years without a shepherd, and were as sheep going astray.

"The hand of God was plainly visible in sending to us, at that important crisis, one whom He had chosen, and peculiarly qualified for our circumstances and needs.

"His ordination was an occasion of thrilling interest to us as a people, and to our newly-chosen pastor, as we have every reason to believe. * * *

"The two and a half years of his ministry was a period of very great interest and profit to this church and people,—made so, mainly, by the consistent Christian influence and wise guidance of our beloved pastor. During the memorable winter and spring of 1858, when the Spirit of God visited this parish, his labors were very arduous and unremitting. Without previous experience, he met all his calls, both public and private, in the most prompt and efficient manner.

"On the first Sabbath in July, 1858, he received into his church, by original profession, thirty-eight members; by letter, nine.* Our young pastor then gave evidence of enjoying to its fullest extent the pleasure of being about his Master's business. Surrounded with these seals of his ministry, he performed the services with the most touching emotions of love, joy, and humility. It had been his constant and fervent prayer that the day might come when many should be added to the church, of such

* The records show 53 added to the church during his ministry.

as should be saved; and now before his risen Saviour, he presented them, and commended them to his care and guidance, with a fervor of spirit seldom witnessed. This seemed his happiest day,—when he could behold the work which had been accomplished for eternity, through '*his feeble instrumentality*,' and in answer to his earnest and agonizing prayers.

"He was encouraged and strengthened, and from that day there seemed to be in him a new power, an inspiration as it were, which never left him through the whole of his brief ministry.

"From the first of his settlement with us, he had been steadily advancing in every Christian and ministerial grace; but the year preceding his death was marked by a rich and sudden development, not only in these graces, but also in mental power, which gave promise of a life of great and increasing usefulness. But the Great Head of the Church has ordered it otherwise. While he has left with us his bright example, his lovely character, the sweet savor of his Christian virtues, to shine on our pathway, he has taken the original, our lovely and beloved pastor, to a place prepared for him among those 'many mansions' in his Father's house above."—*Mrs. G——*, Plymouth.

"Every one noticed his interest in the children of his parish,—his earnest desire that they might be early infolded in the Saviour's arms, and their names written in the Lamb's book of life."

Early in his ministry he wrote thus to his mother: "I mean that the Sabbath-school shall have my first attention." "I have started again the Sabbath-school concert, which has not been regularly held as such for a long time." How well he carried out the above "intentions" parents, whose children enjoyed the benefit of his interest in the institution, best can testify. That his own estimate of its importance suffered no diminution, is strikingly illustrated in the following brief extract from a sermon preached near the close of his ministry:

"How important may be the influence,—

how fruitful in results the fidelity of an humble Sabbath-school teacher! He cannot, even in thought, take the measure of the possible fruit of his devoted labors. With minds around him, destined to act on other minds, and these again on others still, till time itself shall be no more, he seems almost to have other ages placed in his hands to mould them as he will. How unspeakable a privilege,—how responsible a duty! It is not merely the training of the immortal minds before him, important, unspeakably important as this work is, in which he is engaged, but he is shaping the destiny, perhaps, of thousands whom he will never meet or know, till they meet him before the judgment seat of God."

The following brief sketch from his friend Monteith, was addressed to the mother of the deceased, and bears date December, 1860:

"My acquaintance with your son was short, but familiar, if not intimate. We were side by side in the ministry, as you know, for more than two years. During that period, although we were both busily engaged in our respective parishes, yet the contiguity of our fields, and our nimble horses, often brought us together.

"The first time I saw Erskine, after I went to Plymouth, he was engaged in preparing his Thursday evening lecture, and whenever I met him after this (except in our rides), he was earnestly engaged in his Master's work.

"He always evinced an unquestionable love for his work, and made it his first business to secure the faithful discharge of his pulpit duties. He often said he endeavored to make every sermon as good as he could. On Monday, I sometimes found him desponding. He feared that he might have been inexact or unfaithful in presenting the truth, the day before. On such occasions, he used to say his cure was to read one of Spurgeon's sermons, and to reflect how the Lord had blessed performances which made so little pretension to style. His frequent quotations, in conversation, from Edwards, Dwight, Bellamy, Hopkins, and from South and Witherspoon, showed how well he had acquainted himself with the standard theological writers. We have often spent a most exhilarant half hour over some quaint and pithy passage in Bishop South. When we rode on horseback, his spirits were invariably joyous. With the most evident satisfaction he would talk over his plans for future preaching and labor; and I have often remarked his readiness in giving abstracts of the sermons he had preached, or was about to preach.

"I never heard from him anything that indicated an undue aspiration or ambition. He never talked of his future, except as it was connected with Plymouth.

"He was exceedingly attached to the great truths in the Bible, the cardinal doctrines, and the principal events in the life of our Saviour. I used to think he displayed a great deal of skill in the selection of fruitful and striking texts. My people observed his rapid growth from time to time, as we exchanged pulpits. On one occasion, I remember hearing one of my congregation say, 'Brother Hawes brings his sermons right up out of the good book.'

"A few months before his decease, he was deeply interested in a new plan for District Visitation, and Tract Distribution, which his church were about to set in operation. One afternoon he rode over to see me, and said, 'Our church have been praying this afternoon that the Lord would bless this work.' The tears in his eyes showed how genuine and intense his interest was. It was the only time I ever saw him weep.

"In neatness of person, and of everything that concerned his horse or his room, he excelled, almost to a fault.

"When we went to Norwich together to attend the meeting of the General Association, I had an opportunity of seeing more of his private life; I remarked to a friend at the time, that I never had seen a person of so unexceptionable habits.

"The last time I met him before I was summoned to his death-bed, was when he reached me on his return from the General Association in June last. I think this was about two weeks before his death. He drove up to my door, and calling me out, said, 'I have a text for you to preach on: It is the last words of Theodore Parker. He says, I have had great powers committed to me, but I have only half used them. Take these words,' said Erskine, 'and show the contrast between them, and the faith of the dying Christian. In Parker's words, there is a sentiment of self-trust combined with disappointment, and no hope for the future.' Little did I then think I should so soon be called upon to see a sermon preached on this very text, in the triumphant death of your son.

"His death scene, ever calling up the solemn words he addressed to me, the beautiful expressions of filial love and gratitude he gave to his mother, the affectionate remembrances of his father, the sweet hymns he quoted, the firm trust in the words of Scripture, and the bright hope he exhibited,—this scene will remain with me in all its vividness, till I am called to meet him above. For having witnessed all this, I trust, I am, by the grace of God, a better man, a better preacher. I shall ever—with all who knew him—cherish the memory of Erskine Hawes, with the sweetest veneration. Upon whom shall his mantle fall?

"Affectionately yours,

"JOHN MONTEITH, JR."

The mention of his *unexceptionable habits* by his friend Monteith, suggests the propriety of noticing some of his more prominent characteristics. Among these, and the leading one, was the beautiful consistency of his daily life, his conduct and conversation, with his Christian profession.

A friend, who knew him well from early childhood, and who was often with him during his summer excursions, remarks: "Wherever he went, he took his religion with him. Whether among mountain solitudes, far from the busy haunts of man, or in places of more public resort, where all classes are promiscuously thrown together, in their summer gatherings, it shone with the same steady light; never standing out obtrusively prominent at one time, and then, at another, hidden or obscured by worldliness or levity. It permeated his whole character, lending a quiet grace to everything he did and said.

His self-distrust has often been alluded to. This led him to seek that wisdom which cometh from above. Whenever objects of importance were to be effected through his influence, he never trusted to his own judgment, if he could avail himself of the advice of those on whose judgment he could rely. This was strikingly true in his ministerial life.

A neighbor, an elder brother in the ministry, whom he was in the habit of consulting, spoke of this to his parents as something worthy of notice, especially being a *young minister;* such generally feeling better able to direct themselves, than after they have had some years of experience. Then it was the more noticeable on account of the position which he occupied,—looked up to himself for advice, by an intelligent people, by whom he was regarded with a feeling bordering on veneration, it certainly was a mark of humility, and as it proved, of that humility, which the "Lord delighteth to honor."

The lady with whom he boarded during the first months of his ministry in Plymouth, says, "He often came to me in any case where he needed advice; sometimes read his sermon to me, saying as an apology, 'If my mother was here, I should read it to her for criticism, and in her absence, I must make a mother of you,' and if, as in some cases, I suggested any alteration which seemed best to me, as I had been longer in the place, and seen more of his parishioners than he had, he always with the humility of a child accepted the suggestion."

A parishioner, says of him, "In all his intercourse with us, he was a happy combination of the minister and the man."

His natural diffidence never entirely left him. This, with his self-distrust, had rather an embarrassing effect, throwing an air of restraint around him whenever he entered his father's pulpit. It, however, entirely disappeared in his own.

The friend whose remarks are freely alluded to, spoke of this. He says, "I could not but notice the difference between his performances in his own field of labor, and those I had witnessed in his native place. In his own pulpit he spoke unawed by the presence of those venerable men, among whom he had spent his childhood and youth, and by whom he was surrounded when holding forth the Word of Life, in his father's pulpit in Hartford. Although there was never wanting solemnity, and even dignity, yet there was now, an ease and freedom of manner, arising from the feeling, that, to his own people, he was indeed the ambassador of God, to negotiate with them on the high concerns of judgment and eternity."

Having spoken of his *manner* in the pulpit, it seems proper to speak of the *matter* he dispensed from that sacred place. Indeed, the biography of a minister of the Gospel would be incomplete, without some notice of that which constituted his principal work. For this, the subject of this memoir had made no superficial preparation. He had devoted four years to his theological studies, and had availed himself of the best instruction that New England afforded.

When he settled at Plymouth, although he had something of a stock of sermons on hand, he made it a rule to write one new one every week. This he averaged during the brief period of his ministry.

His texts were always chosen with reference to some Christian doctrine or duty, and were happily adapted to the truths he wished to discuss and bring before his people.

His sermons were all carefully studied, fully written out, and are replete with evangelical truth. They were neither the speculations of the learned, nor the fancies of the ingenious, but were "earnest and faithful exhibitions of Christian truth and duty." Such was the testimony of one* who heard him for several consecutive Sabbaths, soon after he commenced preaching. Another, who often heard him after his settlement in Plymouth, said, "He always brings his sermons right up out of the good book."

The impressions made on these two individuals, occupying different positions in society, are such as his preaching usually made on all who heard him.

His preaching, for a young man, took a very wide range, aiming to adapt the teachings of the Bible, to the various characters, circumstances, and wants of his hearers.

He had no hobby, no favorite speculation or theory on which he was continually dwelling, but drawing his subjects directly from the great fountain of truth, aimed so to discuss them, as that they should be seen to be the

* The Hon. Judge Grennell, of Greenfield, Massachusetts.

truth of God, and not the feeble deductions of human reason.

In this way, his preaching was owned and blessed of God, to the accomplishment of the great work of the Christian ministry, the conviction and conversion of sinners, and the edification of Christians in the divine life.

As he approached his end, with the prospect full in view, of soon standing before the Throne, how did the anticipation magnify the responsibility of the preacher's work!—"The Gospel," —"The Gospel in its simplicity"—"This and this only," in its freedom from all taint of human "philosophy"—how did it stand forth in that solemn hour, as the alone divinely appointed "means, for the salvation of a lost world," the one grand theme for the preacher, in the great work of the Christian ministry. With such views, and in such circumstances, how imperfect, how feeble, in his own estimation, did his past attempts in preaching that Gospel then appear.

At one time, near the close of his ministry,

while endeavoring to encourage his people in greater earnestness in Sabbath-school instruction, his mind seemed to dart forward and catch a glimpse of those glorious rewards which await such as have been faithful in the work of saving souls—when he broke forth in words such as follow:

"Oh, how do all earthly rewards dwindle into insignificance, compared with the rewards which await those who have been instrumental in saving souls from death, and bringing them unto glory."

And what are those rewards?

"They that be wise shall shine as the brightness of the firmament, and they that turn many to righteousness as the stars forever and ever. Yea, long after those brilliant orbs have faded and disappeared, they shall shine forth as the sun in the kingdom of their Father."

May we not regard this as a prophetic intimation of what he is now realizing in his own happy experience?

CHAPTER IX.

LAST VISIT HOME—LAST MEETING AMONG HIS PEOPLE.

DURING the third week in June, 1860, he attended the General Association of Connecticut in Rockville, and his home being on the way, he made it his stopping place in going and returning.

He was very desirous of being in Hartford the week following, that he might have the pleasure of listening to Professor Hitchcock's address, at the Anniversary of the Hartford Female Seminary, but the approaching communion and preparatory services, in his own church, required that he should be at home. On taking leave, he said to his mother, "The Fourth of July will soon be here, then I will run home and spend the day with you."

On Tuesday evening, July 3d, he was at his

father's table in Hartford, in free and pleasant converse with his parents. The morning of the fourth was spent in making calls, when he saw an unusual number of his own and his father's friends, not only in their homes, but also in the streets. The light, beaming countenance, the elastic step, and cheerful salutation of that morning, are often referred to.

After dinner, an old and valued friend, once an inmate in the family,* came in, and with him, the subject of this memoir enjoyed a couple of hours of rich intercourse, in which he drew from that learned biblical scholar, much to aid him in his work.

At four o'clock he again walked out, and again, as in the morning, saw a multitude of friends. It seemed as if every one who had known him had a glimpse of his countenance, and a smile from him, on that last day when he was seen in the streets of his native city.

Shortly after tea he retired to his chamber. After he had been there some time, his mother

* Dr. Coleman.

having something she wished to say to him, went up, and on finding the door ajar, entered without the usual signal. He evidently had not noticed her entrance, but sat with closed eyes, apparently in thoughtful meditation. His mother approached, remarking that she saw he was busy, and she would not interrupt him. One sweet look and kind response: "Yes, mother, I *am* busy just now, I am preparing my sermon for to-morrow evening;" and again he relapsed into the same thoughtful posture as before; and his mother left him in deep meditation on the subject which was then occupying his thoughts. The sun had just set, and the softened light as it fell upon those placid features revealed in them a striking likeness of earlier days, clothing them again with infantile loveliness. Whenever that scene occurs to mind, another* is always associated with it, when in that spot, perhaps that very chair, "those soft eyes," and "that upturned coun-

* See earlier page.

tenance" plead in silent, expressive eloquence, an interest in a mother's prayers.

On Thursday morning, at the close of the family devotions, Erskine seated himself directly before his father, and commenced laying open his plans for the instruction and improvement of his people. One, a favorite one, and the last, was this: to prepare a series of expository sermons, from incidents in the Life of Christ; which though interesting and useful to the congregation, assembled on the afternoon of the Sabbath, should be adapted to aid in Sabbath-school instruction. The sermons were to be carefully studied, fully written out, and enriched with such prophetic predictions as should find their fulfillment in the portion under consideration, with other illustrations drawn from the surrounding scenery and circumstances at the time. His father entered with great interest into his plan, and the son with delighted eagerness drank in the instruction that fell from his lips. At the close of the interview, his father said: "My son, if you do this, you will have lived to accomplish a good work." Whenever that scene comes back in memory, the figure that rises before the mind is that of some beautiful flower, opening its petals to catch the morning beams, while yet the dew is glistening in its cup.

After the cheerful "good-bye," and benediction of that morning, that loved voice was never again heard under the parental roof.

A pile of sermon paper, separated from the rest, and divided into compartments, each of which contained the usual number of sheets for a sermon, was found after his death in such circumstances as led to the belief that it was designed for the contemplated series. But another hand was destined to trace other lines across those sheets. Another sermon was to be transcribed there, for the benefit of his people, more effective than any which could have flowed from his own pen,—a sermon, of which, he, himself, was to be the theme,*—an embodiment, as it were, of those Gospel

* His own memoir was written on that paper.

principles so faithfully set forth in the teachings of their youthful pastor, but now more strikingly illustrated in his consistent Christian life, and triumphant death.

That *pile of blank sermons!*—How suggestive!—was there any premonition in the mind of him who placed them there, that his work was done? Their presence there seemed to indicate that he expected to live, and to fill their pages with useful instruction for his people,—and yet there was something in his appearance and manner, and indeed in his whole intercourse with his parents, during that last visit, which led his father to ask, as soon as his son left that morning, "Did you notice anything unusual in Erskine?"

"I did," was the reply.

"He was not melancholy?" continued the father.

"No," was the reply; "he was never more truly cheerful and happy in his life."

Was there not then a beaming forth of that higher life within, which was so soon to be freed from its earthly surroundings, and to find full expansion in its native element above. With the planning of those sermons, his pulpit work was done.

His short but useful ministry is aptly set forth, in some lines suggested by the reading of the memoir of his sister.*

"Oh! not by hours, or full, or few,
Our gracious Lord the toil computes;
Some, ere exhales the morning dew,
At morn retire with sheaves and fruit.
. . . . . And thus did [he]
Whose work . . . . .
Was planned, commenced, and wrought, while we
Beheld it only as begun."

The reader, as did his parents, may feel some interest in knowing what was the subject which so absorbed the mind of the youthful pastor, on that last evening at home. The meeting was held, but that subject was not the theme. The evening was stormy, and but few present, and therefore that subject was deferred until ——. Ah! for how long? "Until the heavens be no more," "when he shall awake

* Rev. Wm. B. Tappan, on reading the Memoir of Mrs. M. E. V. L.

out of sleep" to meet his people,—not a few, on a stormy evening, in that little Lecture-room—but in that vast assembly—every one of them shall be there. He to give account how he preached, and they to give account how they heard, that Gospel which will now be found to have been "a savor of life unto life or of death unto death," to every one of his hearers.

"The scripture selected by the pastor to speak upon that evening, was a portion of the 11th Chapter of the Acts. The subject, 'Steadfastness in the service of Christ.' His remarks were more brief than usual, after which he sat down, saying, 'Brethren, the time is yours.' The meeting then took a conversational turn, the pastor and all the brethren taking a part, asking questions, and giving answers. Our pastor seemed pleased with this, and remained in the desk, protracting the meeting, quite beyond the usual hour. Oh, had we suspected this was to be our last meeting on earth, how gladly would we have remained, 'even until the break of day,' as did the Elders of Ephesus in the days of Paul, listening to the sweet and precious words that fell from his lips.

"In closing, he read the following hymn, and after looking it over, said, 'There does not seem to be any place to divide it, let us sing the whole.' It seems to have been one of his favorites, as he had read it so often as to attract the notice of myself and others. It is a sweet hymn, and the associations connected with it will never be forgotten. It is probably familiar to you, yet I wish to transcribe it all.

HYMN.

(Temple Melodies, Hymn 92.)

God of my life, through all my days,
I'll tune the grateful notes of praise;
The song shall wake with opening light,
And warble to the silent night.

When anxious cares would break my rest,
And griefs would tear my throbbing breast,
The notes of praise ascending high
Shall check the murmur and the sigh.

When death o'er nature shall prevail,
And all the powers of language fail,
Joy through my swimming eyes shall break,
And mean the thanks I cannot speak.

But, oh! when that last conflict's o'er,
And I am chained to earth no more,
With what glad accents shall I rise,
To join the music of the skies.

Then shall I learn the exalted strains,
That echo through the heavenly plains,
And emulate, with joy unknown,
The glowing seraphs round the throne.

"I think he could have selected nothing more appropriate just before his entrance through the eternal gate, to join the innumerable company of angels, the general assembly and church of the first-born, and the spirits of the just made perfect. Farewell, beloved Pastor! How dear thou wast, and art now to us all! Is there not very much to comfort you in the triumphant death of such a son?*

A few additional remarks made by the pastor at that last meeting, seem strikingly

* Communicated by one who was then present.

prophetic of the change but just before him. "He talked of life and death, of Jesus and of Heaven. How well do I remember his tone, and the expression of his countenance, as he said, 'Now we see through a glass darkly, but then we shall know, even as we are known.'"*

We have now carried him through the last evening of health and vigor; the next found him prostrate, suffering untold agony, from the fell blow which in a few hours severed him from life and friends forever.

* Communicated by a young person present.

CHAPTER X.

FATAL ACCIDENT—CLOSING SCENES.

On Friday morning (the 6th of July, 1860), the subject of this memoir rose and addressed himself to the duties of the day with unusual alacrity and cheerfulness. Having finished his preparation for the Sabbath, in the afternoon (as was his wont) he took his accustomed ride, connecting with it a call on one of his most distant parishioners. The ground on which the house stood rose somewhat abruptly from the road, and the only level spot on which the horse could stand was just in front of some bars which secured the carriage entrance to the back yard. On alighting, the strap was buckled around one of these bars. The horse had recently manifested a propensity to pull upon his halter, and in doing so, at the present time, drew out the bar around which the strap was clasped. He was then unhitched and fastened to the gate-post. The ascent here was abrupt, and the only way in which the horse could stand was nearly on a parallel with the fence, and his master being between him and the fence, was obliged to pass quite around him in reaching the gate. In doing this, he gave the animal a light cut with the riding-stick on the hind legs, merely a pat, that he might move out of the way, so that he could pass to the gate. Quicker than thought, the feet of the animal were thrown out, but he was sufficiently removed from those to escape the hoofs. A sweep across the lower part of the abdomen, with the gambrel joint, did the fatal work. He was thrown down the embankment and rolled over into the road, but soon rose and walked into the house. The male members were all absent, and it was some time before any one of them could be found and a physician called. At first, he was not aware of the extent of the injury, but soon intense internal agony revealed its fatal nature.* Chloroform was freely administered as soon as possible, but it was a long time before he could be brought under its influence, so as to experience any sensible relief from his terrible sufferings. The thought of that night almost paralyzes the hand that holds the pen. He was some two miles from home,—and some hours must elapse before friends could reach him from the village. In the morning he was so far relieved as to be moved home. Laid upon his own bed, from which he could look into his pleasant study, his feelings became quite cheerful, and deluded his friends into the belief that he would yet come back into life, and again perform the duties of the pastor among them. Even he, himself, had this hope. He requested his friends to meet and return thanks for his preservation from instant death. The message to his parents contained no request for their immediate presence, but stated that they should be kept in-

* A post mortem examination showed that no human skill could have averted the fatal issue.

formed of his situation, and requested that if possible a minister might be sent out to supply their son's pulpit. It was Saturday. The father had his own pulpit to supply, and as there appeared no immediate urgency, he thought in the circumstances that it would be safe to wait until Monday morning. In the mean time a messenger could be sent, if necessary, the next day. But a few minutes, however, had elapsed ere the mother was on her way, and in a couple of hours was by the bed-side of her son. His voice was cheerful as he welcomed her; but what a change had come over that countenance, which, as it were, but yesterday, she had seen buoyant with health and beaming with cheerfulness! Lest her son should perceive the shock which his appearance had given her, cheering herself, she said, "My son, I have come to stay with you until you are well enough to be taken home." The quick response was, "This is my home; I shan't leave here."

Immediately the friend who was by him,

commenced telling his mother how the thing had happened. Her son had thought she might ask him, and had requested Mr. L—— to do it for him. He commenced, saying, "Mr. Hawes says he don't know how he happened to do that, he had never done it before," alluding to the stroke with the riding-stick. And well he might have said this, as from his childhood he had been remarkable for his caution. The *how* was the last thing in that mother's mind then. The thing was done,—the fatal result was but too visible. But however painful the circumstances, not one of these had taken place independently of an all-wise and overruling Providence.

As the family physician was not at hand, another was taken in during the hasty ride to the cars, and the person who should bring him to Hartford in the morning, could take back the father, if necessary.

On their arrival at the scene of suffering, the attending physician came in. Having spent a few moments with the patient, the two retired to the study. On entering this, the one from Hartford remarked, "What a pleasant study this is. It looks as if it could write a sermon itself. I feel as if I could almost write a sermon here." The patient immediately called out in a clear, cheerful voice, "Dr. ——, I wish you would write a sermon, and stay and preach it to my people to-morrow." There was something so natural, so like perfect health in the tone and accent of the voice, that the pleasing illusion stole over the mind, "he will yet live, he will not die now." But before another sun had set, that voice was forever hushed in death. Even the attending physician, although greatly fearing a fatal issue, was evidently not anticipating so speedy a one. The patient was so calm, so comfortable, and even cheerful, that it was thought there could be no internal injury sufficient of itself to cause death. The thing most feared, and to be guarded against, was the inflammatory process; a few days would decide the case. At the doctor's suggestion, a competent nurse was secured for a few days, and a skillful watcher for the night.

Everything being arranged, and the state of the patient seeming so comfortable, he was left with the watcher, and his mother retired to her room, but soon a note of distress drew her to his bedside, and although all the means and appliances that medical skill could devise were faithfully used, yet it was near morning before the poor sufferer was in any sense relieved.

Not a murmur escaped his lips. Not a regret for anything that had taken place. Only once did he express a wish that anything was different. From the first, his thoughts had often reverted, as it was natural they should, to his Hartford physician. Once during the night, when his mother and the watcher having used all the prescribed remedies and appliances without producing any sensible diminution of the terrible agony, the watcher having gone to procure something needed; he said to his mother, "I wish Dr. —— was here, he would surely think of something to relieve this pain." As he was able to speak, he would suggest with great calmness and judgment what should be done. But the dry, husky breathing, the impeded utterance, and fatal hiccough whenever he attempted to swallow, were but too sure indications that death was doing its work. He spoke once of the night preceding; said to his mother, "he never knew what pain was till then."

Towards morning the sufferer slept—if that state of partial unconsciousness in which he lay could have been called sleep.

His mother retired for a short time to her room. When she returned, she found her son partially raised up in the bed, supported by pillows. He had arranged to be got up, and had ordered clean changes to be brought in. As his mother entered, he said, "I shall be got up and changed soon." She approached the bed, and taking his hand, said, "My son, I think you cannot be got up to-day." The doctor followed and reiterated the same, as he looked upon the pale visage, and heard the weak voice of the patient. He gently bowed his head in assent, and then called the attention of his mother to the perspiration which was covering him. Alluding to this, he said, "I don't know whether it is good;" plainly intimating that he more than suspected the nature of the symptom. The agony had subsided, but it was doubtless owing to the fact, that vitality had ceased in the wounded part. The pulse was fast vanishing. Restoratives were given, but the difficulty of swallowing on account of the hiccough, prevented his receiving much into the system. Great anxiety was manifested by the physician and others, for the arrival of the father. No telegraph offices were open, and there was no hope that the patient could survive until the messenger, who was on his way to Hartford with the physician, should return.

The moisture which covered him, became cold and clammy. Stimulants failed to raise the feeble pulse. No efforts could restore warmth. Everything indicated the hasty strides with which death was approaching.

It is impossible to recall, with anything like accuracy, the order in which the painful events occurred, as also the last remarks, exhortations, and messages, of the youthful dying pastor, during those last brief hours into which so much of effort, and anxiety, and suffering were crowded. But whenever the scene occurs, one fact rises before the mind,—the anxiety and efforts of the attending physician, to preserve vitality in the dying patient until the arrival of his father. How often his watch was consulted, and also the pulse of the patient, as one stimulant after another, or some nutritious restorative was gently given, as the dying one could take them in!

It was past the hour of noon. The painful intelligence had spread over the village. Friends were gathering. He asked for his brother ministers in the neighborhood. Some were then present. Among these, was one whom he loved as a brother, the Rev. Mr.

Monteith. Shocked by the state in which he found his friend, and overcome by his emotions, he wept. Erskine asked him to pray with him. He knelt by the bedside, and with great earnestness and much feeling, commended his dying friend to the Saviour, in this, his conflict with the last enemy. From this prayer, the dying one took in, what had not been intimated to him in words, that death was near. Immediately he asked, "Would it be wrong for me to ask you to pray for my life?" "Certainly not," said his mother. Then he said, "Will some of you retire and do so?" As a few were leaving the room for this purpose, he raised his voice, and said in a clear and emphatic tone, "I want to live, that I may glorify God better in my ministry—I want to live for my people—I want to live for my parents."

Few and broken were the petitions offered. God was signifying his will so plainly, that it seemed to be asking for a miracle, to ask for his life. When the few returned to the room, he was alone with his friend Monteith, and was repeating a stanza in the hymn commencing:

"Rock of Ages cleft for me."

There was a momentary silence, when his mother repeated the last stanza entire, to which he listened with pleased and earnest attention.

"While I draw this fleeting breath,
When my eyelids close in death,
When I rise to worlds unknown,
And behold Thee on thy throne,
Rock of Ages! cleft for me,
Let me hide myself in Thee!"

Mr. Monteith has kindly furnished the substance of the conversation between himself and his dying friend at this time. He says: "After the others had left the room, I waited a little to see if he would try to listen to the prayers, but finding him a little agitated, I said, you have perfect confidence in the 'Rock of Ages?' 'O, yes,' said he, and added: '*Cleft for me.*'

"He seemed a little troubled for breath, and so I began each line, and he finished, with the exception of the last two, which he repeated alone with evident satisfaction. 'Be of sin the perfect cure—perfect cure,' said he—'perfect cure. How blessed that is.'

"He had hardly let go my hand since the first. Now he grasped it firmly, and said, 'Oh! Monteith, remember it,—understand that I say it from this bed,—we ministers have not preached the Gospel in its simplicity. *There* has been *my* error. I want you to understand it that I say it from this bed:—*The Gospel is God's appointed means for the salvation of the soul—philosophy won't do it.*' I will just say, here, that I never had words addressed to me with such emphasis,—they seemed to come from the other world.

"I said to him, 'our hope is secure, for it is an anchor to the soul, and it entereth into that within the veil, whither Jesus our forerunner hath gone.'

"'Ah!' he replied, 'that is not all,—it is *sure and steadfast;*'—and he repeated this phrase several times.

"About this time, I think, Dr. Salisbury felt

his pulse, and said in a solemn tone: 'Mr. Hawes, your time is short,—your race is almost run.' He looked at Dr. S. with an eye steadfast, and that gave evidence of a momentary struggle, and then his face was as bright as an angel's. A change in the activity of his mind, as well as in his conversation, had been apparent for some time. Now his mother asked him if he had any messages to leave for his father. 'O, tell father that I love him. Ask him to forgive me for all the hasty words I have spoken; you know I love you, dear mother, and always have.'"

The following notices are by another hand.

"While he was saying these things, he had leaned partly over to his mother, and was holding his chest, as if the emotions within were greater than he could bear. When laid back upon the pillow, looking upward, he said, '*I want to see father.*'

"Now the doctor wanted him to take some wine. His mother, to encourage him in his effort to swallow it, and in her anxiety to preserve vitality till his father should arrive, said, 'The last you took told perceptibly on your pulse.' Taking her hand in his, and looking her earnestly in the face, he said, 'Mother, I don't want you to do anything to infringe on the purposes of God.'

"He called for brother Averill and brother Tracy, and they were sent for. When the Rev. Mr. Averill came in, he asked him to pray that *this* might be sanctified to his people and his parents; and that the latter might be supported under it.

"As Mr. Averill closed, in a very fervent and solemn manner, he uttered the following petition: 'I pray God will accompany the truth that has been dispensed here for the last three years with his Holy Spirit; that it may be effectual in the conversion of those to whom it was administered.'

"A petition that he offered previous to this, and soon after it was told him that he could not live, was an exceedingly impressive one:

"'I pray God that *this* may be blessed to

the salvation of every member of this family.'

"The family where he boarded had been exceedingly kind to him. They had made him as comfortable as he could have been in his father's house. But they were none of them professors of religion. He felt a very deep interest in their spiritual welfare, had often spoken of their kindness to him, to his mother, and now this last petition for them, went up to the mercy-seat, accompanied with his whole heart.

"It became necessary for his mother to resign her position for a short time at his bedside, in order that something might be done for him, by stronger hands than hers. She placed herself at the foot of the bed, so as not to lose sight of his countenance. Soon his eyes met hers. Fixing them full upon her, with a look of indescribable benignity and affection, he said, 'Mother, I want you to forgive me, and I want you to ask father to forgive me, for all the pain I have occasioned you, for all my hasty words.' His mother, replied, 'You have been a good son, there is nothing to forgive, but if you think there is anything, you are freely forgiven.' How everything earthly seemed annihilated in that moment. The mother stood alone with her son, the last tribunal but just before them—she felt that all must be settled up now. 'My son,' she said, 'I am reminded that I may have something to ask of you; and now I will ask you to forgive me all my unfaithfulness—all my imperfections, in your Christian training.' After saying some kind things in reply, her son continued, 'we all have great imperfections, great sins, but the "blood of Jesus Christ cleanseth from all sin," the righteousness of Christ is sufficient for us all; here I rest, here is my hope; the righteousness of Christ imputed to us. Imputed, that is a good word, I like it.' There was a meaning in this last expression, which those by, who may have heard it, could not take in. The doctrine of imputation had been discussed with much interest, by Erskine and his father, and it was doubtless in reference to conversations on this subject, when his mother had taken a part, that her son now said, 'Imputed, that is a good word, I like it.'

"Changing the theme, he said, 'Mother, you and father have often been in the furnace, but I want you to feel that I am one with you.' Here followed some tender remarks respecting the fellowship of Christians in suffering, with a reference to lighten the affliction coming upon his parents, by an assurance that he was enduring in anticipation, what they would suffer when he should be gone.

"Here, to give a different direction to his thoughts, his mother said, 'My son, you are the Lord's, we gave you to Him.'

"'Yes,' said he, 'and how blessed it is to be the Lord's.'

"The crowd of friends that had gathered, had thronged around his bed. His mother was unable to find a place there. His friend Monteith stood between her and her son. Catching the eager inquiry, 'What is that passage, "We are come unto the city of the living God, the heavenly Jerusalem."' his mother asked for a Bible. One was handed her. She opened to the twelfth chapter of Hebrews, and read, 'For ye are not come unto the mount.' 'Not there,' he said, 'further on.' He then said something which indicated haste, which his mother did not distinctly hear, in her eagerness to catch the right passage, but which those who stood nearest him said was, 'Hurry on to the Prospects.'

"The last syllables were passing his lips, as she commenced, 'But ye are come unto Mount Zion.'

"'There,' said he, 'that's it.' He then took it up and finished it himself.

"Hebrews xii. 22–24, 'But ye are come unto Mount Zion, and unto the city of the living God, the heavenly Jerusalem, to an innumerable company of angels, to the general assembly and church of the first-born, which are written in heaven, to God the Judge of all, to the spirits of the just, made perfect, to Jesus, the

Mediator of the new covenant, to the blood of sprinkling ——'

"Such were the last utterances from lips about to be sealed in death (rather in a more abstract form, than as quoted above) and from the lips of one, who, as we trust, was about to be introduced to that glorious assembly.

"The doctor called for more air. The crowd dispersed. Only his mother, the physician, and one or two friends were left in the room. Instantly he sprang forward in the bed, and throwing out his arms on either side, and looking earnestly around, but with an expression which indicated that he saw nothing within the range of his vision, exclaimed, 'I want to get up, I want to look about.' The doctor's arms were instantly around him. 'Mr. Hawes, we will raise you up in the bed, you can sit up and look around here.' Pillows were placed, his head fell forward upon his breast. When laid back upon the pillows his eyes were set, and all appeared motionless, as if death had already done its last work. But, not so. The 'dying strife' had but just commenced. The first groan sent his mother backward a little space; but soon recovering herself, she was again by the bed of death. Every breath was now a groan—and the fearful sound was heard distinctly for some distance without. As soon as his mother had sufficiently recovered herself, she lifted the covering from his arm, which lay motionless by his side. It was livid and cold. Perceiving the fingers to curl slightly, as if cramped, she took the hand in hers, and attempted to straighten and warm it. Immediately he raised it, and commenced rubbing his breast. His mother now did this for him; but whenever she ceased for an instant, in order to take a dry part of the cloth she was using, for the perspiration was profuse, he immediately raised his own hand and continued the rubbing until she commenced again. He would then lay his hand down as intelligently as in health. Thinking he might possibly hear, his mother repeated portions of Scripture: only one is remembered. Taking the lead from his utterances, she repeated, 'They have washed their robes, and made them white in the blood of the Lamb.'

"At length, nature worn out and exhausted, the painful groans ceased. The breath became soft as an infant's. Then the purling sound of the purple current within, and one soft rush of breath, gave note that the deathless tenant had escaped its clayey tenement, and all was repose.

"Those eyes out of which he had looked so lovingly, on parents and friends, and through which so much of the beauty and grandeur of these lower works of God had entered, to gladden and to adorn the immortal mind within, and those lips, through which so much of God's saving truth had been proclaimed to dying men, now sealed and rayless in death, were closed by loving hands.

"'So he giveth his beloved sleep.'"

The next view his mother had of him, he was sleeping peacefully in the centre of that "pleasant study," on the table at which he had daily sat and meditated on those solemn and weighty truths, of which he was now experiencing the reality. Only the Sabbath previous, his theme had been, "The Transfiguration." Was he not now beholding that glorious vision realized? Not as then, dimly shadowed forth to the eye of faith, but amidst the ineffable brightness of heaven.

There he lay, so calm, so peaceful, as if he were only "taking of rest in sleep." "Lord, if he sleep, he shall do well." Could not this have been said of the sleeper there, with a deeper meaning, than when uttered by the disciples to their Master, respecting one whom he loved! It is matter of grateful recognition to the mother of the deceased, that, that *last look*, always takes precedence of the painful one at the same hour of the afternoon previous, whenever her mind turns to the death of her son.

A veil must be drawn over the scene on the arrival of the father. Doctors Knight and

Salisbury were there to receive him, but human sympathy was powerless then. Having assisted him into the house, they seated themselves in silence by his side. That most appropriate and expressive act was appreciated, and afterwards spoken of, by the stricken father. The following morning his parents returned to their home in Hartford.

It had been arranged that the funeral services should be attended in the church at Plymouth, on the Tuesday following,—and the same in his father's church in Hartford, on Wednesday morning.

On Tuesday evening, at six o'clock, his remains were brought home to his father's house in Hartford, accompanied by the delegation from his father's church, who had attended the funeral obsequies in Plymouth, and also a few of the Plymouth people, among whom was his friend Monteith.

Another hand than the writer's could better describe those funeral solemnities in that church, where the deceased lay, on the very spot where twelve years before he had stood, and in the freshness and vigor of youth, had devoted himself in solemn covenant to God; and just beneath the font, with whose baptismal waters, his parents, in early infancy, had done for him the same.

A large delegation of the church in Plymouth were present, and mingled their sympathies with the parents and friends of their youthful, deceased pastor.

Addresses were made by the ministers with whom he had associated in Plymouth and vicinity, among whom were his friend Mr. Monteith, Rev. Mr. Averill, and Mr. Tracy. Mr. Webber, also, pastor of the North Church, in Hartford, and who had known him in the Theological Seminary in Andover, gave a very pleasant tribute to his memory.

The prayers, the hymns, the music, were of the most appropriate character. The first hymn,

"Peace, 'tis the Lord Jehovah's hand,"

had often soothed the father's grief, as one

after another of his children had been taken from him; and now it appropriately came in as a healing balm for the last wound of the kind he was ever to receive.

The last hymn:

> "Hear what the voice from heaven proclaims,
> For all the pious dead,"

seemed but the utterance of Apocalyptic benediction, "Blessed are the dead who die in the Lord."

A select company of his young friends in the ministry gently laid him down in his last resting-place; then a few members of the choir of his father's church, with whose voices his own had often united, sung that beautiful and appropriate him of Tappan's:

> "There is an hour of peaceful rest."

After which, the Rev. Mr. Spring, of East Hartford, said a few consoling words, and offered a brief prayer over the open grave, and the precious dust was closed from sight,—but not forever. "It shall rise again in the resurrection at the last day." Bursting the cerements of the grave, it shall come forth, not as now, subject to decay and death, but purified from everything earthly, and "made like to Christ's glorious body."

ADDRESS BY THE REV. DR. SPRING.

It would appear to be more in the course of nature that the aged, who had finished their work, should precede, on their way to the grave, the young and vigorous who have apparently many years of activity and usefulness yet before them. And such a fact corresponds with our experience. And when we find it otherwise, when the young die before the old, and disperse all the hopes which had gathered about their early years, as we ask for some solution of the problem, we are reconciled to the disappointment only by the reflection that there are wise and good reasons, perhaps yet to be disclosed, for the perplexing anomaly.

If we enter a grove where trees are standing of every variety of age, and beauty, and use, we are not surprised to see the aged and full-grown that have long kept their place, and have blessed whole generations with their shade and fruit, cut down and removed, that place may be given to plants of promise whose fertility and beauty are yet to adorn the enclosure. It is the ordinance of a wise and good Providence. They have accomplished their destiny, and there is nothing in the arrangement that excites surprise. But when the axe is laid to the root of a young and beautiful tree of whose growth and maturity the most pleasing anticipations had been formed, we are perplexed, and we wonder what ruthless destroyer has been there. We feel like grieving and complaining over the work of desolation. But our perplexity is at once relieved when we are told that the Proprietor has ordered the removal, and especially if he has transplanted the favorite to adorn his own personal residence, where its beauty and promise shall be to his lasting honor and gratification.

So in the removal—untimely, as we are

prone to estimate things—of the beloved youth whose remains we now consign to the grave, all our surprise is checked by the remembrance that the Lord of the vineyard has been here. This transfer has not been made without his direction. What though the tree under whose shadow a Church and Congregation would have sat with great delight and whose fruit would have been sweet to their taste, shall bloom no more on earth, it is but transplanted to the Paradise of God to flourish in immortal fragrance there.

We are "dumb and open not our mouth, because thou, O Lord, hast done it."

CHAPTER XI.

BRIEF NOTICE OF FIRST MEETING BY HIS BEREAVED PEOPLE—LETTERS OF CONDOLENCE—EXTRACT OF REPORT OF CHURCH—SERMONS.

MANY touching notices of the church prayer-meeting on the evening of the day succeeding his burial, were sent to the parents of the deceased pastor, by the members of his church. One writes:

"I have just returned from our Thursday evening prayer-meeting. One short week ago, our pastor was with us in our little lecture-room; but how changed was everything to-night! Our steps echoed as we walked along the lonely aisle, and how heavy were our hearts. The bell commenced ringing—I cannot tell you the feelings of that moment. Our pastor always used to step in before it ceased. Then we all sat and waited,—waited for what? We knew too well that he never more would cross that threshold,—never more would look round upon us with beaming countenance, as he was wont, when stepping into his accustomed seat,—never more would read to us from that sacred volume which lay unopened on the desk, never more would feed our souls with heavenly manna.

"When the hymn was read all were too much overcome to sing,—we were wont to hear such a sweet voice strike off at once. Now all was silent. At the close of our sad meeting, there was no one to pronounce the benediction over our heads, unless, indeed, our glorified pastor looked down in pity from his bright abode and blessed us ere we parted." * * *

The fourth Sabbath after his death was a memorable one to that church and people.

Resolutions, expressive of their submission to the divine will in this trying dispensation, also of the deep sense of their loss, and their high appreciation of the character and labors of their pastor while with them, concluding with an appropriate and tender testimonial to his memory, were presented "to the whole church and congregation assembled on that Sabbath." A letter from the parents of the deceased was read, and a hymn on the death of the righteous, by Montgomery, was sung by voices with which his own had often mingled:

HYMN. (664, CHAPEL HYMNS.)

THIS place is holy ground;
World, with thy cares, away!
Silence and darkness reign around,
But lo! the break of day:
What bright and sudden dawn appears
To shine upon this scene of tears!

Behold the bed of death,—
This pale and lovely clay!
Heard ye the sob of parting breath!
Marked ye the eyes' last ray!—
No!—life so sweetly ceased to be,
It lapsed in immortality.

Could tears revive the dead,
Rivers should swell our eyes;
Could sighs recall the spirit fled,
We would not quench our sighs,
Till love relume this altered mien,
And all the embodied soul were seen.

Bury the dead and weep,
  In stillness o'er the loss;
Bury the dead—in Christ they sleep,
  Who bore on earth his cross,
    And, from the grave, their dust shall rise
    In his own image to the skies.

One who was present said, "It seemed like attending his funeral over again."

In the afternoon, a sermon on Home Missions was read. The young pastor had finished it just before taking that fatal ride, and had expected to preach it on the coming Sabbath; and as he regarded the subject as one of paramount importance, he had taken great pains in its preparation. The circumstances in which it was presented to the people, doubtless contributed much to the effect produced. The collection taken up was much larger than ever before for the same object.

The heavy draping was kept upon the church, with its motto wrought in white silk, in front of the pulpit, for nearly two months:

"He being dead, yet speaketh."

Before its removal, the following impromptu

lines were found in church, written on the blank leaf of a psalm-book:

WHY should these sable curtains hang
  Around this house of prayer?
No gloom is resting o'er his grave,
  No shadow lingers there.

No funeral badges hang around
  His home in heavenly light;
We know his ransomed soul is clad
  In robes of purest white.

'Twas but the prison walls that fell
  Beneath death's mighty stroke,
Why should we mourn for one released
  From earth's oppressive yoke?

Why should we grieve that one prepared
  Has entered into rest?
Why should we weep for one who leans
  Upon the Saviour's breast?

A letter of sympathy, written by the subject of this memoir, to a friend in affliction, was returned to the mother of the deceased eight years after it was written, with the following note:

"Dear Madam,

"I cannot but call to mind, that while your honored and loved son was with us, he early learned to sorrow with the afflicted. A letter of condolence from his pen, dated Andover, November 2d, 1852, now lies before me. May not the words of the son fitly come back to comfort the parents, now that they are bowed in grief at his loss!" It read thus:

"Dear H——, I regretted, exceedingly, that I could not tarry in Hartford, to mingle my grief with yours, and drop a tear of sympathy over the remains of our dear departed friend; but I rejoice to think that you can resort to a far better source of consolation than mere humanity can afford,—to him, who, when on earth, wept at the grave of Lazarus, and whose watchful eye in heaven numbers every silent tear. You are not left to sorrow as those without hope, but you may expect at some future day to sing the glories of the Lamb, with him whose voice you will no more hear on earth. How delightful, too, and how illustrative of the sufficiency of the Christian's support in death, that the departed one so calmly entered the dark valley, in the unclouded use of reason, and with songs of praises* on his lips. I have often, of late, repeated to myself those beautiful lines in the Village Hymns:

> Before we quite forsake our clay,
> Or leave this dark abode,
> The wings of love bear us away
> To see our smiling God.

We cannot tell what visions of glory the dying Christian may behold, just as the thread of life is parting, and the curtain is being lifted, which separates the unseen from the seen.

"But while we delight to follow the spirits of our departed friends, in our conceptions, to the world of light, we should not forget to learn the salutary lesson of our own frailty.

"How solemn the admonition falling from the lips of the living with almost prophetic force, and now from his silent tomb: 'Be ye therefore ready also, for in such an hour as ye think not, the son of man cometh.'†

* "Sing, sing," he said; but voices of friends were choked with grief, when he commenced a favorite hymn, and sung till his voice was lost in death.

† Lesson for his class in Sabbath-school, when he was in health on Sabbath morn, and on Wednesday morning, following, was no longer here.

"I can scarcely restrain a tear when I recur to the pleasant scenes of last summer, those mutual communings with nature in all her loveliness and silent grandeur, in which it was our delight, but, now, our melancholy pleasure to have participated; but viewing the matter in another light, there is, if not cause for joy, yet reason for consolation. He is now no longer witnessing the ever-fading scenes of earth, but the constant, unfolding glories of heaven. He has done with earth,—its pains, its sorrows, and its sins,—and has been admitted, as we trust, to 'the innumerable company of saints and angels;' and what is more, to the joy of God's immediate presence. Here let us leave him, hoping, ourselves, at some future day, to be accounted worthy, through the merits of the Lamb, of the same blessedness.

"With kindest sympathy, I am very sincerely yours, E. J. HAWES."

From Mr. W. B. Capron, long associated with the deceased on terms of intimacy, first in his father's house, at Hartford, then in the high-school, and last at Andover.

From his far distant home in India, he writes to the mother of the deceased:

"I have been dwelling upon the circumstances connected with your bereavement, which should bring you consolation. But my mind runs back to the years of my acquaintance with Erskine; and yours will run back, no doubt, to the years of his youth and his childhood. It is a great blessing to you to have received such a treasure from the Lord, for so many years, and with so few drawbacks; and while you will love to linger upon the evidence of his growth in grace, and his active usefulness during the years that he labored in the ministry, I am sure you will take scarcely less pleasure in remembering his fidelity in study, and in his duties as a teacher, his diligence, his self-distrust and yet real ability, his excellent taste, his skill in music, in composition, in mechanics also, his sociability, his kindness,—in fact, his well-balanced mind, and well-balanced heart, which you saw in him, and saw to be appreciated by others.

"I remember the years of my acquaintance with him, with great pleasure, and have been instructed and reproved, while my heart has been touched by this story of his last hours."

The following from the Rev. Mr. Gulliver, of Norwich, is a very graphic and truthful delineation of traits, which friends who best knew him, have often seen in him:

"At Rockville,* your son sat for some hours opposite me in church, and my eye rested on him for a long while, attracted by the peculiarly earnest, tender, I may say, *beautiful* expression of his countenance. I thought how wonderful it was that one accustomed to such a position from his childhood, accustomed to see his father a leader in the church and among the churches, should be so modest and retiring, so ready to hear rather than to talk, so much more inclined to do, than to direct.

* At the General Association of Connecticut, a few weeks preceding his death.

How little did we think that those lovely qualities were so soon to adorn the circles about the throne of God and the Lamb! and that that sweet spirit was to find society and sympathy among the angels of God! But so it is. And there is a more delightful thought still, that now the young disciple whom Jesus loved is leaning his head upon the Saviour's breast, and with his missionary sister, now walks with him in white. I cannot fully and only condole with you, that such children have gone before you to welcome you to heaven. I must also bless God that he has given you such children, and congratulate you that you have been able to give them first to the church, and then to heaven."

The following is from a respected friend of the father of the deceased,—a man of position and influence in society:

"I can never forget (in my own somewhat similar bereavement) the very delicate, unexpected sympathy I received from your beloved son. Such was his modest and gentlemanly bearing,—such the refinement and sympathy of his character,—as the result of his fine education and training,—and all this adorned with a sweet and unaffected savor of piety, that he was my decided choice for our late vacant church. But God, in infinite wisdom, has transferred him to higher and nobler service in His upper temple."

The following from the Rev. Professor Fitch, of New Haven, strikingly illustrates the affectionate sympathy which he awakened in friends towards himself while living, and which his premature removal called forth towards his stricken parents.

"I remember your earlier griefs over Louisa* and Thomas, long since put to rest in their little graves. And Mary, so long a light and joy in both our households, whom we gave away as the bride of a missionary to an Eastern land, who has long since laid her to rest, near the shores of the Bosphorus. But Erskine remained. We have followed him in his course

* "Louisa, My First-born:"—S. S. Union.

of studies and preparation. We have seen him welcomed to the ministry of the Gospel. He was testifying to the love of Jesus before a people appreciating his ministry. We saw in him, we trusted, a friend to survive us in our old age, and bear our memory with him to another generation. It seems but yesterday he passed a day with us in our family, cheering us with his society, and receiving joyfully our counsels and the 'God speed thee' of our hearts. And is he gone? Erskine, very dear wast thou to our hearts. Your Lord and Saviour knew better what to do with you and for you than we. In His hands we leave you in submission and hope."

"REV. DR. and MRS. HAWES.

"My dear Friends:

"The following lines were penned after reading Dr. Tyng's account of the last hours of your son, in the 'Independent,' and after hearing a sermon preached by my faithful pastor, Rev. Mr. Thurston, of Fall River, alluding to the same event, and particularly to those thrilling words:

'HURRY ON TO THE PROSPECTS.'

"Hasten mother, onward hasten!
Soon my soul from earth must part;
Tell me of those glorious prospects
Which await the pure in heart.

"Hasten, mother, onward hasten!
Fast my life doth fainter grow;
Tell me of that heavenly fountain,
Whence the *stream of life* doth flow.

"Hasten, mother! onward hasten!
Hear I now those songs of praise,
Sweetest music heard in heaven,
Music which the ransomed raise.

"Hasten, mother! hasten quickly!
Tell me of the sprinkling blood,—
Tell me of Celestial Mansions,—
City of the Living God!

"Edward Buffinton.

Fall River, Mass."

Extract from the Annual Report of the Centre Church, Hartford, for the year 1860.

"But we cannot forbear alluding to one, whose sudden and untimely death sent a thrill of sorrow through the city of his birth, and filled this house to overflowing with sympathizing and weeping mourners.

"Rev. Erskine J. Hawes was well known among us. He was loved and esteemed by all. None uttered a syllable against his character. Even in his youth he was of singular purity, sincerity, obedience, and discretion. We watched him with anxious interest as he passed into manhood. In college, and in the theological seminary, he maintained the same consistency of character, and came out at length fully equipped for the arduous duties of the profession which he had chosen. He added to a vigorous mind and sound judgment the acquirements of a ripe scholarship. Thus accoutred he went forth with quiet courage, to make conquests for Jehovah. And how manfully and successfully he continued the warfare against Satan's kingdom, let his brief ministry at Plymouth answer. Here he began a career of extended usefulness, and rapidly developed in mind and heart. He became prominent in advocating public reforms, and was already beginning, in no small degree, to mould the public sentiment in the town to which the Providence of God had called him. As a preacher, his aim was more and more to set forth 'Christ and Him crucified.' As a pastor, he endeared himself greatly to all the members of his flock. Already, in the short space of two and a half years, more than fifty had renounced the world, and enrolled themselves under the banner of Jesus. But suddenly the stroke fell! Oh, the blighting of fond hopes, the sundering of tender ties, the grief of whole communities, the abrupt ending of a useful life, the going out of a star in the heavens! The going out? Ah, no! It set behind our sky, only to glow with more effulgent radiance in the galaxy of heaven!

"But it is well. Revelation and reason conspire to teach us that it is well, when the Christian dies. Our brother has, indeed, gone from our sight; he has 'hurried on to the prospects:' but he has left with us 'the treasures of [his] well-spent life,' the fruits of his short but successful ministry, and the fragrant memories of his triumphant death. And we will say of him, and of the other loved ones, whose graves are still fresh among us,—

> "With us their names shall live
> Through long succeeding years;
> Embalmed with all our hearts can give,
> Our praises and our tears."

CONSOLATION IN AFFLICTION.

A Discourse

DELIVERED IN THE FIRST CONGREGATIONAL CHURCH, IN HARTFORD, JULY 15, 1860, BEING THE SABBATH AFTER THE INTERMENT OF THE REV. E. J. HAWES, PASTOR OF THE FIRST CONGREGATIONAL CHURCH, IN PLYMOUTH, CONN.,

By J. HAWES, D. D.

DISCOURSE.

"For as the sufferings of Christ abound in us, so our consolation also aboundeth by Christ."—2 CORINTHIANS i. 5.

THE sufferings referred to in the text were such as Paul and his associates in the ministry were called to endure for Christ's sake, or in seeking to promote his cause in the salvation of men. They arose from the opposition and hatred of enemies, and from persecution, trial, and want. These the Apostle had to encounter in large measure, and in various forms, in the whole course of his ministry. But in proportion as he suffered for Christ, his consolation abounded through Christ; the one was set over against the other, or rather the one was far more abundant than the other; and all, as he tells us in the verses following our text, redounded to the glory of Christ and the comfort and edification of those to whom he ministered. Whether we be afflicted, he says, it is for your consolation and salvation which is effectual in the enduring of the same sufferings which we also suffer, or whether we be comforted, it is for your consolation and salvation. And our hope of you is steadfast, knowing that as ye are partakers of the sufferings, so shall ye be also of the consolation.

But it is not my purpose to discuss the subject suggested in the text in this its broad and general character, but to confine my remarks to the sufferings which come to us in the form of bereavement in the loss of near and loved friends by death. In this view let me invite you to consider with me, on the present occasion, some of the sources of consolation open to us under the bereavements and trials of life.

It will at once occur to you, my friends, that the scenes of the past week have forced this subject on my attention. It occupied my thoughts, indeed, while on my lonely way last

Sabbath afternoon, to the house, which was even then, though unknown to me, a house of mourning. And since my return, with all the sad mementoes of death and the grave pressing on my mind, I have scarcely been able to turn my thoughts to any other subject than that suggested by our text as the theme of present meditation. I shall not, of course, consider it in special application to myself, thus obtruding my own personal sorrows upon public notice; but I shall endeavor to set it before you in its general aspect and bearing, in the hope that you may be the better prepared for bereavements and trials when they shall come upon you. And come they will, in one form or another, to all whom I now address. There is no exemption. Affliction and sorrow are the lot of all that dwell in the flesh. We are born to trouble as the sparks fly upward; and sooner or later the bitter cup is passed round and pressed to the lips of all living. Some individuals, indeed, and some families, seem almost an exception,—they have lived so long with nothing to interrupt the steady flow of prosperity or break in upon the circle of domestic happiness. But such cases are rare; and I have long since learned to look upon them, when they occur, with painful apprehension. I know the tide must turn, and when the stream begins to flow in an opposite direction, it is common, as I have observed, for wave after wave to roll in, in quick succession, breaking up long-cherished connections and sundering long-endeared ties. Trials, it has often been remarked, seldom come alone. They frequently tread quick upon each other, as in the case of Job, and none are more likely to be visited with this experience than those whose sun has long shone brightly upon them, and few if any clouds have passed over their path. But however this may be, it certainly becomes us all, in a world like this, to remember the days of darkness, for they will be many. And when or how soon they will throw their shades around us, we cannot tell. The brightest prospects may be suddenly overcast, and our dearest earthly enjoyments may be swept away in an hour, and in a manner entirely unexpected by us. Trials lie hidden along every pathway in life, and they often come upon us when we least think of them, and in a form to stir the deepest sensibilities of the soul. Indeed, it is like God to conceal the hand that moves the mighty wheels of his providence, and to strike in a manner to make himself regarded. He gives none account of his ways, and often his bereaving stroke falls as lightning from a clear sky, giving no warning till the work on which it was commissioned is done. A father, a mother is suddenly smitten down; a husband, a wife is snatched away; a loved child of many hopes and many prayers is hurried from the stage of life in the midst of his days and his usefulness; and the whole story of the sad event is told in one word,—he is gone. So the fashion, the pageant of this world passeth away. Nothing permanent, nothing fixed and certain. We know not what a day may bring forth. We only know that we live in a world of trial and change; that our fairest prospects may suddenly be darkened and from the enjoyment of large happiness and long-unbroken prosperity, we may in a moment be summoned to the sorest bereavements and the bitterest sorrow.

Exposed thus, as we all are, to these sad reverses, to these sinkings in the deep waters of adversity, how important that we should all know, while yet the ways are smooth, and no dark cloud appears in the horizon, what sources of consolation and support are provided for us to which we may resort when days of bereavement and trial shall come. To point out to you some of these is what I shall now attempt:

1. The great fact which underlies all that I have to say on this subject, and essential indeed to all true consolation under the afflictions and trials of life, is, that an all-wise and benevolent Providence presides over the affairs of men and regulates all the events of time. Without the recognition of such a Providence this would, indeed, be a dark world,—all given

over to chance; no plan, no wise purpose controlling the course of events, and no presiding power to direct them to benevolent results. But, blessed be God, it is not in such a world that we live. Much as there is in it that is dark and mysterious to us short-sighted mortals, the great truth stands before us in the clear sunlight of God's word,—the Lord reigneth, and true and just are all his ways. His providence, bearing the impress of his own perfections, is infinitely wise, benevolent, powerful and good; and it extends to all creatures and all events. It is universal, taking in the whole creation; it is also particular, directing the falling of a sparrow and numbering the hairs of our head. And it is a providence which never errs, which never fails, but always does just that, and only that, which is wisest and best; best adapted to show forth the glory of God and promote the highest good of them that confide in Him, and are owned as the children of his love. Sustained by this blessed truth, we may lift up our hands and our hearts, amid the darkest and most trying circumstances in which we can be placed,—and exclaim,—The Lord liveth, and blessed be my rock, and let the God of my salvation be exalted. There is a light above the cloud that now seems so dark and heavy: soon the light will break through the cloud, and it will pass away, and all will be cleared up and made plain. This remains an unfailing, ever-enduring source of consolation in any situation in which we can be placed. Nor is it any deduction from the all-sufficiency of this precious source of support that the providence of God is a deep unfathomable to us; that it is often wrapped in darkness, and subjects us to trials which seem wholly mysterious, which we cannot explain, and which we sometimes feel we cannot bear. God governs for the universe, and He governs for eternity. It is of necessity, therefore, that his ways in our view must often be in the great deep, and his footsteps not known. We can see but little of that vast plan which God, in the dispensations of his providence, is executing for his own glory and the best good of them that love Him. Enough is known to lay a perfect foundation of trust and hope. We have only to wait a little, leaning on the arm and confiding in the love of an ever-present and all-perfect God, and soon all will be made plain. What we know not now we shall know hereafter; and it will, I doubt not, be a part of our delightful employment in heaven, inspiring us with ever new gratitude and praise, to study the evolvings of God's providence towards us in this world, and the means he saw fit to use to fit us for his service on earth, and for the everlasting enjoyment of his presence in heaven.

2. It is another source of consolation under bereavement and trial, to reflect that they are a necessary part of the discipline of life; the appointed and the essential means of developing character and fitting the soul for a higher and happier state of being. If man were in his primeval state of innocency, as in paradise, he might not need the discipline of adversity

and sorrow to keep him near to God, in obedience to his will, and in growing fitness for his presence and glory. It might then be safe for him to enjoy uninterrupted happiness, as it is for the angels and for the redeemed in heaven! But man is no longer in innocency; he is in a fallen, sinful state; we all partake of the effects of the apostácy, and are inclined from our earliest days to forget and forsake God, and to choose the vain things of earth and time as our portion, to the neglect of the great interests of the soul and eternity. This is the malady, the moral malady of our entire race. Nor is it wholly removed by that change of heart which brings us to repentance and to Christ our Saviour. Far from it. The disease of sin, in some of its many forms and workings, still cleaves to us, and the discipline of suffering seems necessary to carry on the process of cure and to effect our entire restoration to spiritual health and fitness for the kingdom and service of God. And this, we are abundantly taught, is one great end designed to be accomplished in us by the afflictions and trials of life. And they seem absolutely necessary to this end. We can none of us bear uninterrupted prosperity. It is not safe for us. The discipline of unbroken comfort, if I may so speak, is too soft and tender for such indocile, self-willed creatures as we are. It acts unfavorably and hurtfully on our higher, spiritual interests. It tends to form a hard, unsympathizing, selfish and worldly character. "It is," says Evans, "upon the *smooth* ice we slip; the rough path is safest for our feet. The tearless, undimmed eye is not to be coveted here,—that is reserved for heaven." We need trials now, afflictions, sorrows, many and of various kinds, to keep us in our place; to make us what we should be, and to educate and train us up for a higher state of being hereafter. Our Father in heaven knows this, and, therefore, in paternal love and faithfulness, he subjects his people to the discipline of suffering; he casts them into the furnace; bereaves them of their loved ones; lays his hand heavily upon them, and all, that

He may purify them, draw them nearer to Himself, and make them larger partakers of his holiness and of the joys of his salvation. And it surely is a great source of consolation in our bereavements to know that God is designing our good by them. And good they will certainly do us if we receive them in a Christian manner. They are adapted and intended to stir the deep sensibilities of the soul, to show us our weakness and our dependence; to draw forth our purer and better affections; to inspire us with tenderer and more active sympathies; to engage us in a closer walk with God, and to make us more like our blessed Saviour, of whom it is testified, that even he was made perfect by suffering,—that is, a complete Saviour, suited in all respects to our character and wants,—made such by the things he endured while here in the flesh as our elder brother. And how interesting to hear it said of him, now that he lives and reigns in glory, *he can be touched with the feeling of our infirmities, our sorrows, having in all points been tried* as we are; and, a most consoling truth it is, ever to be borne in mind in the midst of our trials, that we have a merciful and faithful High-priest ascended for us into the heavens, one who is able to sympathize with and to succor us in our sufferings, having suffered himself, and been made perfect, fitted completely for his office, as Redeemer and Saviour, by suffering. Yes, it is true, as a tried, experienced sufferer once said,—"Christ has gone through every class and grade of our wilderness school;" and how should it console and reconcile us to our lot to reflect, when trials are heavy upon us, that he is conducting us through the same school in preparation for an eternal residence with him in the mansions he has prepared for us in glory?

3. It is another source of consolation under the bereavements and trials of life, that, when borne in a Christian manner, they always come mingled with peculiar tokens of God's presence and love. So the Apostle found it in his experience. As his sufferings for Christ abounded,

so also did his consolation in Christ. The Saviour came near, and sustained and comforted him with his special presence, with his supporting grace, with his love shed abroad in the heart and the joys of an assured hope of heaven. No one can read the writings of Paul without being struck with the fact that his purest joys, and his brighest hopes, and sweetest songs, were closely connected with scenes of deep trial and suffering for Christ. Nor was his experience in this matter at all peculiar to him. It was common to all the primitive disciples of our Lord. In proportion as they endured trials and sufferings in the cause of their Saviour, he came near and blessed them with his presence and favor; they took joyfully the spoiling of their goods, were patient and happy under the loss of all things, and went singing and triumphant even to the gibbet and the stake. And so, in all ages: the Saviour has come nearest to his friends in their seasons of affliction and trial;—they trusting in Him; and has given them peculiar manifestations of his grace and love. He may not, indeed, remove the cup nor prevent the bitterness of the draught, but he supplies needed strength to the inner man, imparts peace and joy and hope to the smitten spirit, and often gives a realization of his nearness, of his friendship and presence, never enjoyed in an equal measure at any other time. They find it, indeed, to be true,—as thy day, so shall thy strength be. When the three friends in Babylon were cast into the burning, fiery furnace, one like unto the Son of man was seen walking with them in the midst of the flames, guarding them from all harm. So when the Christian is cast into the furnace of affliction, he is sure not to be left alone; if he bows to the dispensation and trusts in him who appoints it, one is sure to be with him mighty to help and to save, and his presence and favor are more, infinitely more than a compensation for the loss of all earthly comforts. How often has it been witnessed that Christians of true piety have found their happiest seasons of communion with God and the sweetest hours of spiritual enjoyment, just when their afflictions were heaviest and their trials the most severe. "Oh," says one, "I thought I could never bear such a trial as has come upon me; it seemed to me in prospect that I should sink under it and die; but it came; I bowed to the stroke; I said, the will of the Lord be done,—and He was near to me, and held me up and gave me such tokens of his presence and of the glorious fullness of his grace as I never knew anything of before." Oh, that this may be our experience, my beloved friends, when called to drink of the bitter cup of affliction and sorrow.

4. It is yet another source of consolation under the trials of life, that they are but for a moment, and then will be succeeded by everlasting blessedness in heaven. Weeping may endure for a night, but joy cometh in the morning. For our light afflictions, which are for a moment, work for us a far more exceeding and eternal weight of glory. And in another place the Apostle says, For I reckon that the

sufferings of the present time are not worthy to be compared with the glory which shall be revealed in us. And again, No chastening for the present seemeth to be joyous, but grievous; nevertheless, afterward, it worketh the peaceable fruit of righteousness unto them which are exercised thereby. Oh! this *afterward;* it has long seemed to me a term full of deep and comforting significancy. When the blow that sweeps away our comforts first falls, it often stuns us, as it were; we are overwhelmed by it, and it seems more than we can bear. But soon a soothing, softening process begins, bringing peace to the soul and fruits of righteousness, sweet to the taste even now, but far sweeter when fully ripened in heaven.

We are prone, indeed, as I know from painful experience, to think of our trials when fresh upon us, as too heavy to be borne, and we are ready to imagine that there is no relief from them, and no end. But this is our weakness. Rightly viewed, we shall deem them light and momentary, as the Apostle did his trials. This is, indeed, their proper characteristic,—light and but for a moment. They are light compared with what we deserve; are light compared with what others, better than ourselves, have suffered; and light, because, if we bear them aright, God helps us to sustain them, enabling us to cast the burden of them on Him, with the assurance that He will comfort and uphold us. There is yet another circumstance that makes our trials light,—they work a healing process in our souls, dislodge us from our earthliness and sins, and bring us into a nearer conformity to God, and a greater fitness to appreciate and to enjoy his grace and love. And then how true it is that they are but for a moment? In their first bitterness they dash every cup of enjoyment, as it were, with gall, and spread gloom over all the prospects of life. But soon, time, with the grace of God, comes in with a softening, sustaining hand, blunts the keen edge, and breaks off the sharp points of our bereavement, and leaves us with the happy fruits that spring from it to cheer and refresh us on our earthly pilgrimage. But even should our bereavements and trials be many, and should seem to follow us in quick succession all along life's journey, still we may say of them, and truly, they are but for a moment. They will soon be over; we part with them as we pass over Jordan, to enter the celestial city, and shall meet them no more forever. And how near is that time! But a step, and we reach the end of our earthly course and earthly trials, and all beyond is everlasting blessedness. In the place to which we go, if we are Christians, there shall be no more tears, no more death, neither sorrow, nor crying, nor any more pain in the sundering of ties that unite kindred and friends. There all that is now dark in the dealings of divine Providence will be cleared up. Eternity will show how *all*, *all* was needed, that came upon us here; that nothing else, nothing less, could have done. "With all its mazy windings and rugged roughness, the way in which Christ is leading us on, if we are his, is not only *a* right way, but *the* right way, the best which covenant wisdom and love could select." So we shall find it in the final result,—the winding up of this checkered, intricate earthly scene. And how consoling a truth is this to rest upon under the trials and sorrows of life? "Nothing," says Jeremy Taylor, "does so establish the mind amidst the rollings and turbulence of present things, as both a look *above* them, and a look *beyond* them; above them to the steady and good hand by which they are regulated; and beyond them, to the sweet and beautiful end to which by that hand they will be brought." With this precious truth shedding its light and comfort into our souls, we may well say with one of old, in every dark and trying day,—though he slay me, yet will I trust in Him. Would, said an eminent Christian, now entered on his rest, that one could read and write, and toil and pray, and suffer and compose one's self to sleep, as with the thought,—soon *to be in heaven*, and that forever and ever. I must mention:

5. One other source of consolation under the bereavements of life,—it is, that, when called to part with near and loved friends who die in the Lord, our separation from them is but for a brief time. They have gone just before us over the narrow stream, and are waiting on the shining shore to welcome our arrival, to join their happy society and intercourse, to part no more forever. They have gone from us; but they are not perished. They are still alive,—alive with all their powers invigorated, with all their affections purified, with all that was lovely and interesting and good in them here made perfect; and clothed with immortal youth and vigor, they remember us, pilgrims on earth, with a warmer love than ever, and are looking and longing, it may be, for the day when we, too, shall quit these scenes of mortality and go to be ever with them in the presence of their and our Lord and Saviour. Yes, we shall surely meet our dear Christian friends in another world, and shall know them and love them, and

forever enjoy their society. I have the deepest conviction of this truth. It is fully sustained in the scriptures; it is most reasonable in itself, and accords well with all that we know of the soul and of the scenes of immortality beyond the grave. And it is a truth which grows sweeter and more comforting to my heart every year I live. I lean upon it and bring it home to my bosom with fresh gratitude and faith in this day of my sorrow. My son, my dear and only son, thou art gone to the grave before me, hast left me a lonely mourner in the decline of my age; but I would not recall thee, to renew the battle of life, and pass through the agonies of another death-scene. No, the last conflict is over, the victory is won, and thy Saviour, I trust, has taken thee to Himself to serve and enjoy Him in a higher sphere of activity, of usefulness and blessedness than earth could afford. And there thou art waiting for thy parents, now mourning thy departure, and weeping over thy too early grave, as it seems to us, in our short-sightedness. But thou wilt not wait long; we are nearing the brink of the river over which thou hast passed, and ere long the summons will come for us to launch away, and go to the spirit-land where we confidently hope for thy welcome, and to have thee near to us forever. And, tell us, hast thou found thy loved brothers and sisters who died before thee? Were they ready to greet thee, when, bidding us farewell, thou didst pass so suddenly within the vail? Yes; ye are all together now, and ere long, as I humbly hope, we shall all meet, a happy, united family, to minister to each other's joy and blessedness in the presence of our Saviour, and to the glory of his rich grace forever and ever. Yes; and other thoughts crowd on my mind, as this prospect opens to my view and sheds its light and comfort to cheer my afflicted, bleeding heart. There, on the distant shore, toward which I am fast sailing, I see dear departed friends, in large number, to whom I ministered while they were yet with us, and whom I loved as followers of the Lord Jesus and fellow-helpers in the gospel,—I see *them waiting*,—the nine pastors, too, that have labored and died here before me, and the happy ones whom they assisted on their way to glory,—yes, all waiting to welcome me and others belonging to Jesus of this communion, to their society, and to the general assembly and church of the first-born in heaven,—there, all accounted worthy of this blessedness will finally meet and have a grateful recognition of former friendships, and of each other, as disciples of the one common Saviour,—parted here for a season by the unsparing hand of death, but reunited now in a purer, happier, perfect love, to dwell together forever, with no fear or possibility of severance during everlasting ages. This is a prospect which may well sustain and comfort us as, amid changes and trials, we go on to finish our course on earth. The end will soon be reached, and beyond shines one eternal day; there God, the sun, forever reigns and scatters night away, and lost ones restored to our embrace will be taken from us never, no never.

I have thus, my friends, speaking from a sorrowing, smitten heart, indicated to you some of the sources of consolation opened to us in the loving-kindness of God, and to which we are invited to have recourse in seasons of adversity and trial. I commend them to you, my dear people, in the earnestness of a pastor's love and a pastor's care. Many of you may not feel the need of them now. I see you here to-day in health and happiness; parents surrounded by their children, no one of their number missing; and happy family circles that have never yet been broken in upon by death, nor clothed in garments of mourning. But the past is no security for the future, nor are present happy circumstances any pledge of what will be to-morrow. I stood here last Sabbath, urging upon you the duty and privilege of prayer, and though not without anxiety from what I had heard the afternoon preceding, I had no apprehension of what was passing on a bed of suffering in the home of one dear to me as life, or that within a few hours I should be written childless. But so it was, and while you were assembled here for worship, I was on my way to the place of bereavement and sorrow. And in my loneliness and great fear of what might be before me, I tried to console my feelings and prepare for the mournful issue, by dwelling on the thoughts I have now laid before you. Take them to your bosoms, my beloved friends; you may soon have need of them; know what the sources of consolation are while yet the hand of bereavement is stayed and the cup of sorrow is not pressed to your lips. It will be no time to discover them or to find your way to them when the blow has fallen and you are crushed by its weight. Let the great truth of an all-wise, overruling Providence ever be present to your minds, your stay and support in the day of trouble. Learn to look upon the trials of life as disciplinary, educational, adapted and designed to detach you from the world and to fit you for a higher and happier state of being. Ever be prepared to meet trials, in a state of mind that will bring God near to you; a very present help in trouble, on whom you may cast your burdens and find Him ready to sustain you. When afflicted and tried in the death of near and loved relatives and friends, remember that these afflictions are but for a moment, and the separation which you now mourn will soon be followed by an eternal reunion in heaven.

These thoughts which I thus commend to you, I have found precious to myself in this day of my sorrow. Would that I could bring them nearer to my heart, and draw from them more abundantly the consolation they are fitted to afford. I cannot but feel under the stroke that has fallen so heavily upon me. The heart smitten will bleed, the fountain of tears unsealed will flow. I know who has done it, and though I know not now why He has done it, I doubt not that He had wise and good reasons, and that what now seems so deeply mysterious and trying, has upon it the character of a Father's love, and I shall yet see it.

Still the thought is a bitter one,—*I was a father, and I have lost all.* Of six children, not one lives to call me by that endearing name. The last is gone, laid by the side of four others, while a fifth lies entombed on the shore of the Bosphorus,—separated *here*, but united *there*, and there I hope ere long to meet them.

After what you heard at the funeral exercises last Wednesday, I deem it unnecessary, and it might seem improper, to say much touching the brief life and sudden death of my dear son. I may, at another time and in another form,* perhaps, say something of him more particular. He was born and trained here in the midst of you. He was baptized in this church. For many years he was a member of our Sabbath-school. Here he professed his faith in Christ; here he worshipped and communed at the table of the Lord; and here he has often stood to preach the Gospel and commend to you the Saviour whom he loved. I am happy to think of him, as having, in the whole

* That has now been done by a mother's hand.

of his brief course, maintained a singularly pure, untarnished character, sincere, open, kind, honest and unassuming in all his intercourse with others, winning from them a willing tribute of confidence, affection and respect. Happily settled in the ministry, loving his people and loved by them, he was, in the estimation of all who were best acquainted with him, especially in these latter months, fast increasing in mental vigor, in warm, earnest piety, in devotedness to his work, and in all the qualifications which promised to raise him high as a faithful, efficient and useful minister of Christ. These things were noticed by his parents, by his people, and by his brethren in the ministry, who had the most intimate intercourse with him; and I was happy in the thought, that, while I should have him to lean upon in my declining age, he would remain to preach the Gospel to his fellow-men, when I should be silent in my grave. But he is gone, and I am left alone. But, blessed be God, I do not mourn as one that has no hope. The summons to depart, though coming suddenly, found him not unprepared. His Saviour came near to him in the agonizing, dying scene, and he uttered many words of strong faith and hope, as well as of calm submission and peace. These, dear departed one, we accept as thy last precious legacy to thy sorrowing parents and friends, and as comforting pledges of soon meeting thee again in the happy home whither thou hast gone before us. Henceforth, I would learn from the suddenness as well as from the peace of thy death, to prepare the better for my own; happy if, reminded by these changes and this decaying strength of the frailty of my life and of the account I must soon give of my ministry, I may be ready for the summons. Deprived of all my children and left alone, as it were, in the world, with none to stay up my steps or bear my name to a coming generation, henceforth I would "devote to the flock, which I have to feed with the word of life, the remnants of a voice that falters and a strength that is fading away."

NO NIGHT IN HEAVEN.*

"There shall be no night there."—REV. xxi. 25.

THE views which men entertain of heaven are very apt to be modified and colored by their own peculiar temperament and habits. It is said of the late William Wilberforce of England, that he loved to think of heaven as a place of rest; and the reason of it was, he was a man ever burdened with cares, and for many years was incessantly harassed and oppressed with the toils and responsibilities of public life. He wanted rest. On the other hand, Robert Hall loved to think of heaven as a place where there should be no more pain; and the reason in his case was, that, during the greater part of his life, he was

* It will at once be seen that the occasion of this discourse was the same as that of the preceding. Both grew out of a scene of bereavement and sorrow, and they are now published in the hope that the sentiments they contain may afford light and comfort to some when called to drink of the bitter cup.

subjected to extreme bodily suffering, and often to the most excruciating torture. But the idea of heaven presented in the text is more general and comprehensive than either of these. It denotes freedom from darkness, or obscurity of mental vision; and from all perplexity, suffering and trial. The term night as used in the text, is a figurative expression to denote exemption from whatever is obscure, intricate, mysterious, and trying in our present state of being. It is often so used in the Scriptures, and also in common discourse; and accepted in this sense, it will help us to form some views of the heavenly state, which, to some present at least, it cannot fail to be interesting and instructive.

It is well remarked by the excellent Richard Cecil, that "though the word of God furnishes a minister with a rich variety of topics, yet his discourses will be much influenced by his feelings, and colored by his own experience. Is he a man strong in faith and buoyant in spirit? like one standing upon a mountain, he will naturally discourse to others of the firmness of the foundation on which he stands, and will describe to them the beauties of the prospects around him. Does he, on the contrary, tread the valley of tears? he will then naturally become the companion of the afflicted, and point out to them what he himself learns in the vale." Placed as I am, in the providence of God, in this latter state, amid the shades of night that have gathered around me, and the swelling of deep waters through which I am called to pass, my thoughts naturally seek relief by turning to scenes above and beyond the things of earth and time, to that pure and happy heaven, of which it is said in the text, "there shall be no night there." Let us dwell on this thought. There is much in it to sustain and to animate, while, as pilgrims, we sojourn in this dark and mysterious state of being. It is night now; but it will be full, bright day hereafter. Let me mention a few things which properly characterize the present as our night state. Here we see almost all things, especially such as relate to spiritual objects, through a dark, imperfect medium. We think of God, for example, the great first cause and upholder of all things. Wherever we turn, we see evidence that such a being exists, and we cannot but feel that in Him we live and move and have our being; Himself, everywhere present, independent of and ruling over all. But how little do we know of this invisible, mysterious, almighty Being? How deep the night that hides Him from our view; veils his character and ways from our scrutiny and our comprehension! Canst thou by searching find out God? canst thou find out the Almighty unto perfection? It is as high as heaven; what canst thou do? deeper than hell; what canst thou know? The measure thereof is longer than the earth, and broader than the sea. There is no searching of his understanding; no comprehending of his mysterious, unfathomable attributes or the eternal counsels of his infinite mind? Enough is known to lay a perfect ground of confidence and hope; but oh, how little, in this our night state, are we able to comprehend of that infinite, eternal Being, who reigns in high authority over all worlds, orders all the changes of life, and holds our immortal destiny in his hands?

I have referred to the counsels of God, to the plans and purposes of the infinite Mind. These embrace the universe in all its parts, and extend to all creatures and events. But how little do we know of them; how profoundly are they concealed from our view; hidden in the bosom of the Eternal, so that we can know nothing of them, only as they are developed in providence or are faintly shadowed forth, in some of their parts, in the book of revelation. God gives no account of the designs and purposes according to which He governs the world; and they are enveloped in deep night till they are brought to light in the movements of that mighty Providence which foresees, pervades, and rules over all.

And then this Providence — what a deep unknown; what a sea unfathomable is it to us! Look back and read the history of the past, and how much do we discover which seems to us profoundly mysterious and utterly inexplicable in this our night state of being! How different a world is this from what we might expect to proceed from the hand of such a being as God, and how differently has it been and is governed! Whence came sin and all the misery and woe which have overspread the world for six thousand years? If God is infinitely powerful, how easily might He have prevented the evils under which our race has so long groaned, and suffered, and died! If He is infinitely wise and good, why did He not do it? So we reason, and yet we are confronted by stern facts, and our reasoning is naught. This whole subject is wrapped in deep mystery. I see no way to explain the difficulties involved in it. The facts are before me. I feel their sad pressure on my spirit, and I see their crushing weight as they fall upon my fellow men. But no ray of light comes to disclose to me the reason why sin came into the world; why the earth is strewed with the dying and the dead, and why such multitudes are left to live and die in their sins, and be lost forever. It is night, dark night in my view in relation to all that is connected with the existence of natural and moral evil, and the terrible consequences that are to result from this state of things in a future world.

Then, if we look at the course of events, as developed in God's providential government of the world, how much there is in it that is dark and mysterious! how entirely unlike what might have been anticipated from the known character of God! We know that He is a Being of infinite wisdom and mercy, and loves to communicate happiness to his creatures; yet we see them everywhere sunk in ignorance and sin, oppressed with calamity, surrounded by miseries, and we find that man has, in all ages and conditions, been born to trouble as the sparks fly upward.

A way has been opened in the Gospel for the enlightenment and salvation of man; and from the known design of God in providing a Saviour, and the all-sufficiency of his grace to meet the deepest wants of our race, it might have been expected that long, long ere this, centuries ago, the tidings of salvation would have been proclaimed through the earth, and all have been recovered from the power and misery of sin and restored to the image and favor of God.

But how very limited, as yet, is the knowledge of the Gospel, and how little has been done by its light and power, compared with what might have been anticipated from the divine principles it contains, from the character of its author and the interest it possesses in the heart of God! How dark, how inexplicable is this fact: God's great remedy for the sins and woes of our race known only to a small part of mankind, and that after a lapse of more than eighteen hundred years. A great part of the world is no better than if Christ had never come to save lost men, and the Gospel had never been proclaimed. Many who hear it are even the worse for what they hear; for where it is not a savor of life unto life, it is a savor of death unto death.

I might here refer to many of the doctrines of Scripture, and show that while they are sufficiently clear and full to guide and assist us in duty and point out for us a safe way to heaven, there is much, very much in them which we do not comprehend, and which, while in our present state, must always appear obscure and mysterious.

But I have time only to notice further the obscurity of providence, its dark and intricate dealings with ourselves. If we look to our past, how many things in our history are wrapped in night: we can give no explanation of them. They came upon us suddenly, unexpectedly, and we knew not till an unseen hand was upon us, leading us into unknown paths, and in ways entirely hidden from our view. And if we turn to the future; what do we know of it? It is all veiled in obscurity. We cannot see a step before us, nor know what a single day or hour may bring forth. This only we know that changes and trials await us; for they are the common allotment of all; but in what form and at what time they will come upon us is known only to Him in whose hand is our life and breath, and whose are all our ways. Oh, as we cast an eye along the path that is to conduct us to the grave, how little do we know what is to befall us; how unseen the descending stroke of affliction and bereavement; how hidden is the time and manner of our death, and how deep the night that hides the scenes of eternity from our view, except only as by the light of faith and hope we may anticipate that we shall find the favor of God through Christ, and enter into a state of everlasting blessedness.

I might expatiate much more on this part of my subject. But let us pass to consider that this night state of our being, as I call it, is to be succeeded by one of bright, everlasting day. There shall be no night there. The reference here is to heaven—the world of perfect purity and everlasting blessedness, revealed as the future home of all the redeemed of the Lord. Of that world we can, in our present state, have but a very imperfect conception. The fact that there is a holy and a happy heaven prepared as the future abode of the righteous, is clearly made known to us in the Scriptures. It is a *place;* a place of infinite magnificence and beauty; forever illumined by the presence of God, and adorned with all that is suited to satisfy the purest and noblest desires of our immortal minds, and to advance us forever in knowledge, in holiness, and happiness. Still our conceptions of heaven, in this dark and shadowy state of being, must of course be exceedingly inadequate. It is of necessity represented to us under sensible images, or images drawn from sensible objects with which we are here familiar—grand and beautiful indeed, and yet as used to set before us spiritual things, must fall far short of the reality. Several of these images are presented to us in the context. Heaven is there spoken of as a vast city, with walls and gates and streets of pure gold and pearl and transparent glass. John, who had a vision of it, says: "I saw no temple therein; for the Lord God Almighty and the Lamb are the temple of it. And the city had no need of the sun, neither of the moon to shine in it; for the glory of the Lord doth lighten it, and the Lamb is the light thereof. And the nations of them which are saved shall walk in the light of it, and the kings of the earth do bring their glory and honor into it. And the gates of it shall not be shut at all by day, for there shall be no night there. And they shall bring the glory and honor of the nations into it. And there shall in no wise enter into it anything that defileth, neither whatsoever worketh abomination, or maketh a lie; but they which are written in the Lamb's book of Life." Now all these are obviously figurative expressions, designed to give us the fullest and most impressive conception of heaven and its glories of which we are now capable, but which, no doubt, comes far short of the reality, and may, in many respects, as it lies in our minds, be very unlike the reality. Thus in regard to the expression in our text, "There shall be no night there;" it is, as before intimated, to be taken in a figurative sense; and thus viewed, it means, not merely that there is to be no literal darkness in heaven, but nothing of which night is the emblem—no obscurity, no perplexity, no calamity, or sorrow, or bereavement, no dark, mysterious providences of any kind to try our faith and cast their shadows on the future. It will then be all day, all bright, unclouded light. *Here* is our night state. *There* night will have passed away forever, and clear, full day will shine upon us for eternal ages. *There*, there will be no night in regard to the character and perfections of God. For He is the sun of that world, and his glory doth lighten it for ever and ever. And they need no candle, neither the light of the sun; for the Lord God will shine forth there in all the glory of his attributes; will manifest himself *as He is* with such clearness and fullness of light as will scatter all the darkness that now hangs over our minds in regard to his being and perfections; for, as the Scriptures assure us, we shall dwell in his presence, shall see Him as He is, see Him, face to face, and know Him even as we are known. Our minds, too, freed from all the weakness and obscurity that attend us in this our fallen state, and made equal unto the angels, as we are assured they will be if we are found with the redeemed in heaven, we shall be qualified to know God as now we cannot, and to apprehend the glory and excellence of his character and ways, far, far beyond what we can at present have any conception of.

Then, too, there will be no more night in regard to the purposes of God, his government, and his plan of salvation for lost men. This world's great drama will then be closed; the design of God in its creation and government accomplished, and all that is now dark and mysterious in relation to this subject will be cleared up. We shall then see, certainly far beyond what we now can, why sin was permitted to enter this world, and with it the sufferings and woes of so many thousand years. We shall then see why ignorance and idolatry and crime, and all the influences that combine to make men miserable and fit them for destruction were suffered to hold so long and fearful a sway on earth, and that too, notwithstanding the full provision made in the goodness and mercy of God for the recovery of the lost to his favor and kingdom. This whole subject, wrapped in profound night now, will then have shed upon it the light of perfect day, amid the revelations of the heavenly state. God will then be seen in the glory of his holiness, his justice, his truth, and grace; his throne will stand vindicated before the universe, his ways towards man fully justified; Himself loved, adored, and praised as worthy of the supreme homage, obedience, and trust of all intelligent beings.

There will be no more night there in regard to the providence of God, as administered over the affairs of man, often now veiled in deep mystery. All will then be cleared up, and it will be seen that God had wise and good reasons for all the events which we were called to experience in this state of probation and trial. It will then be seen why so deep a veil hides future scenes from our view, so that we cannot know what a day may bring forth, nor be certain of life either for ourselves or others, a single hour or moment. We shall then see why the young, the vigorous, and the promising of long life and usefulness in the world are often called away in the midst of their days, while the feeble, the sickly, the wicked, and the useless are spared to be a burden to themselves and a sorrow and grief it may be to others. We shall then see, too, why we are so often tried, disappointed, and crossed in our pathway in life; why our favorite plans are disconcerted, our brightest hopes darkened, our most loved treasures taken from us, and we left, as it were alone, to tread our solitary way to the close of our earthly course. All these things, now so inexplicable and trying in this our night state, will all be explained in the light of that day, which is to shine with no night forever, in the mansions of heaven. There will then be found *a need-be* in respect to the darkest and most trying events that befall us in life; and we shall then *know* what it is now so hard for us sometimes to *believe*, that our severest trials are mercies in disguise, and that our light afflictions, which are but for a moment, work for us a far more and exceeding weight of glory, while we look not at the things that are seen, but at the things that are not seen. Under the hand of God, all the events of time, all the afflictions, changes and to trials of life, are carried forward to give place or to be united with that which is now unseen and eternal. This is the development of the whole plan, the explication of all the intricate movements of Providence. Look at the things which are unseen and eternal; there is the state to which we are tending, and there we shall know in perfection what we now know only in part, and shall be satisfied that all has been conducted in infinite wisdom and goodness, so as best to illustrate the glory of God, and secure the highest happiness, present and eternal, of them that love Him. In heaven there will be no night in regard to the mode of our entering that world, and our immediate condition on arriving there. We shall then have passed through the change of death and the grave, and have entered the celestial city, living, conscious, active beings; and though, as Isaac Taylor well suggests, in his Philosophy of a Future State, it may take some time to adjust ourselves to our new state of being, and to the new laws of intercourse and action prevailing around us; we shall know that we are at home in heaven, free from sin, from sorrow, from death; spiritual beings in the midst of a spiritual world; surrounded by beings like ourselves, in eternal harmony with them, with God and all the holy subjects of his empire. There will be no night there in regard to the recognition of departed friends. We have reason to believe that on leaving this world, we shall enter at once into the society of loved ones who have gone to heaven before us, and that we shall know them, and be known of them. *How* this will be in our then changed mode of being and circumstances, it is not easy for us to conceive; but it will be plain hereafter, and friends will greet friends, in mutual recognition and love, to part no more forever.

There will be no night there in regard to the manner of holding intercourse with the redeemed of the Lord, and other beings of higher order than ourselves; or in regard to what is to constitute our and their employments in the heavenly state. We know we shall be active there, shall be able to pass from place to place with the greatest ease, and shall be occupied ever in ways perfectly suited to our immortal natures, and adapted to carry us forward forever in knowledge, holiness, and happiness. At present, however, much obscurity rests on these points. We view them as objects of faith, revealed for our comfort and hope in this state of our earthly pilgrimage; but the full vision and position of them are reserved for that world where there is no more night. There all these things will be known; known in our own happy experience and to our everlasting joy and blessedness in the presence of God and the Lamb. All darkness, all obscurity, all perplexity trial and sorrow will have fled away forever; and we shall have before us the bright and glorious prospect of eternal progress in all that shall assimilate us to God and fit us for the society and employments of angels and of glorified beings before his throne.

The subject thus presented suggests many deeply interesting reflections, but I have time only to touch upon a few in the briefest manner, leaving you to follow them out at your leisure and to apply them to the practical concerns of life. And,—

1. There is good reason for the saying of the patriarch of old,—I would not live always. Not that this world has no sources of consolation and enjoyment. It has many; and if we were always in a state of mind to use them right, no day of our life would pass, but we should have fresh occasion for thanksgiving and praise for the goodness and mercy shown us by our Father in heaven. But this world was never designed to be our home. It is not the place of our rest; we are soon to leave it; and while we remain in it, the trials and changes that we meet with, or witness around us, are fitted to remind us that this is our night state, that we have here no continuing city, but should seek one above where reigns bright, eternal day. Better things than earth contains are provided for us in heaven, and with these in prospect, we may well take up the language and say, as we pass along, I would not live always. Who would wish to grope in perpetual night, when by passing through a door he might enjoy full, bright day? or who

would wish always to conflict with the imperfections, the sins, the trials and sorrows of this life, when he is invited to enter herein as his eternal home, and there be blessed with perfect freedom from all the ills of this probationary state, and enjoy complete, everlasting happiness in the presence of God his Saviour. This world, too, even in its best form and highest enjoyments will grow old, and after awhile lose all its attractions. In Madame de Stael's memoirs of her father we have this striking remark: "I have a proof, says Mr. Nester, of the immortality of the soul in this, that it is at least, after awhile, desirable, and essential to our happiness. By the time we have reached three score years and ten, we have looked around us and become familiar with the whole scene; and though not *satisfied*, we are *sated.* Then we feel our need of a new residence, a new sphere of activity, and new sources of employment and enjoyment." This is a striking remark, and duly impressed on the mind, we can hardly refrain from exclaiming in the beautiful language of the hymn:

> "Who, who would live alway, away from his God,—
> Away from yon heaven, that blissful abode?
> Where the rivers of pleasure flow o'er the bright plains,
> And the noon-tide of glory eternally reigns?
> Where the saints of all ages in harmony meet;
> Their Saviour and brethren transported to greet;
> While the anthems of rapture unceasingly roll,
> And the smile of the Lord is the feast of the soul."

2. Christians have good reason, when they come to die, to meet the change with cheerfulness and hope. They exchange night for day, sin for holiness, sorrow for joy, earth for heaven. They leave a world of darkness and sin for a world of unclouded light and perfect holiness. They leave a world of ignorance, error, sorrow and death, for a world of perfect, unerring knowledge, and of everlasting blessedness. That world is entered by the change of death,—a change not indeed without its pains and terrors, but transient and quickly over, and when passed, the Christian enters at once into a state, "where all things are as sub-

stantial as here they are vain; where all things are as momentous as here they are frivolous; where all things are as great as here they are little; where all things are as enduring as here they are transitory; where all things are as fixed as here they are mutable; where, in a word, God shines as the eternal sun, and pours the light of his glory and blessedness upon all the inhabitants of that holy and happy world. Well might the Apostle, in the faith and hope of such a world, say, I am in a strait bewixt two; I desire to go and be present with Christ, yet willing to remain, if it be God's pleasure. But welcome the day of departure, the hour of sweet release from this my night state and of my introduction to a state of clear sunshine and everlasting day. So every true Christian has good ground to feel and to say, when called to meet the change of death.

3. Our subject furnishes strong ground for submission and consolation in the loss of friends who have died in the Lord. They have gone from us, we miss them in the family circle and

in the intercourse of life, and a thousand things occur to bring them fresh to our memory, and to remind us that we shall no more see or converse with them in this world. And then the heart will bleed, and the tears flow afresh. It is not wrong to feel our loss and mourn when loved ones are taken from us and we are to see them no more as we pursue the lonely journey of life. But there are sources of consolation here which we may not overlook. Our dear departed friends who have died in the Lord,—where are they? In that world where there is no more darkness; where all is light; where shines one unclouded, everlasting day. There they are freed from all the imperfections, weaknesses, temptations, sins and sorrows of this life, and transformed perfectly into the image of Christ, they behold his glory, dwell in his presence, and are entered into the mansions prepared for them in their Father's house above. They are now satisfied; all that was dark, trying to them, in this world, is cleared up; the book of Providence is now unsealed to their view, and every page of it, however obscure and mysterious here, is now read in the light of heaven, and every word and letter of it is seen to have been inscribed by unerring, everlasting wisdom and goodness. And themselves who once walked in darkness here and saw no light, are constrained to exclaim,—He hath done all things well. Marvellous are thy works, Lord God Almighty: just and true are all thy ways, O thou King of saints.

So it is with all our friends who have died in the Lord and entered into heaven. And should not this satisfy us, and more than satisfy us? Should it not even call forth our thanksgiving and praise? They have left us for a little while; have reached the goal and gained the crown for which they strove in life, and now victors in the presence of their Saviour and King, they wait to welcome us to their society and to their rewards in heaven forever. Wherefore, my brethren, comfort one another with these precious truths. Some of us feel the need of this comfort to day; others may soon feel the need of it, for the cup of sorrow is passing round and to whose lips it will next be pressed, we know not; happy will it be for us if when called to part with friends, we can think of them as passed into the world where there is no more night, and where we may hope to meet them when the time of our departure shall come.

4. Prospects ineffably glorious are before us, if we are indeed the disciples of Christ and heirs of his kingdom. The present night state in which we live will soon pass away, and with it all obscurity, perplexity and trial forever, and instead will dawn upon us, a day which has no night, a day of eternal sunshine, of revelation, and glory and blessedness in the kingdom of our Father and Saviour. This prospect is before us, it hastens on apace, and soon, if found faithful, we shall realize it in all its glory and blessedness. As this world passes away, another opens to our view. This prospect enlivens the solitudes which bereavement and decays of nature produce. This prospect be-

comes a substitute for the scenes and charms which have faded and fled. This prospect entertains and engages, when the days are come in which we say, I have no pleasure in them. The outward man perisheth, but the inward man is renewed day by day. Our heart and flesh fail, but God is the strength of our heart and our portion forever. We depart, but we leave what is not our rest, what is dark, unsatisfying and passeth away,—while we enter a creation where everything that is new, and grand and pure, and attractive and beautifying, says,—Arise and come away. And the hour that obscures and quenches forever all other glories, raises us, if Christians, to immortal life and blessedness in heaven. But, oh, if not Christians, not disciples and followers of the Saviour in a life of faith and love and devotion to his service, the reverse of all this will come upon us,—and instead of the sentence,—Come, ye blessed of my Father; inherit the kingdom prepared for you from the foundation of the world, we must hear the fearful doom—Depart ye accursed into everlasting fire prepared for the devil and his angels. An awful alternative; it is set before each one of us: in view of it we are called each one to make our choice for eternity.

CPSIA information can be obtained
at www.ICGtesting.com
Printed in the USA
LVHW040429110522
718423LV00002B/390

9 783375 001186